THE LAND UNDERSEA

Glas Awyddn smiled wanly. "At first," he said, "Where I walked, the land to either side of the river was open. But as the river slunk forward the grassy slopes gave way to bracken and then to a wood. I went on warily. Now and again a chill light flickered between the boughs. Then all at once, something flashed in the river.

"Turning my head, I saw there was a man standing alone in the flood. He was leaning hard on his spear. His sword and his armor were as red as his hair.

"*You are in dear straits, Glas Awyddn*, he said. I looked and I felt a loneliness sucking close to my heart.

"The Redd Man watched me. *Unless I carry you*, he said, *You cannot cross*. He was silent a little. *Nor will I carry you unless you first give me the thing that I ask. For here is the only way into Tir Fo Thuinn. Since the beginning no lord has ever gone in or gone out of it except with my leave.*

"For another space there was silence. Then I said quietly, *It will not be a small thing that you want*.

"*To some it is little*.

"*And to you?*

"*Have you loved?* said the Redd Man.

"I stood stiff on the bank. *Once*, I said but the dread of that answer caught fast in my throat. *Tell me the price*, I said hotly.

"*No more than one drop of your heart's blood*, he answered, his voice a whisper.

"*Come then*, I murmured. *If you will have it, you will not have it idly*.

"*Nor did I mean to*, he said. And as he spoke he cast his great spear . . .

Bantam Spectra books by Paul Hazel

YEARWOOD

UNDERSEA

UNDERSEA

Volume II of *The Finnbranch*
Paul Hazel

mre deep

with

Paul Hazel

BANTAM BOOKS
TORONTO · NEW YORK · LONDON · SYDNEY · AUCKLAND

UNDERSEA

A Bantam Spectra Book / published by arrangement with
Atlantic-Little Brown & Company Inc.

PRINTING HISTORY
Atlantic-Little Brown edition published November 1982
Bantam Spectra edition / September 1987

Prologue

This is the second book of The Finnbranch. The first book, *Yearwood*, told of the early manhood of Finn, who, when Yllvere gave birth to him, was given no name. His mother and her women were the Kell, of the lineage of the Selchie, the spawn of sealmen and shorefolk. They were witch women, living apart and in dreams in a house called Morrigan on the side of the highest mountain in the North or West. Long after the whiskered and webfooted men left them and went back to the sea the women still pined for them. Finn was the son of the last of the sealmen to come up on the land, but this his mother hid from him along with his name— for the boy was not the child of her husband.

In the month of his birth, in April, Finn went walking in the forbidden wood on the mountain. There he found and climbed the god-tree, Gwen Gildrun, whose vast branches spanned many miles. At the tree's summit a crow pecked out his eye. Though half-blinded, he brought two fledgling crows away with him. Vydd, his mother's sister, stole them and taught them man-speech. From her Finn learned a part of the mystery of his birth. From his mother, in her deep cell under the house, where nightly she kept great fires burning the root of the god-tree, he learned that another child had been born with him, that his mother's dark servant, Tabak, had taken the child. But no more than that would she tell him.

Unsatisfied, Finn set out from Morrigan seeking his birthright. Tabak rode with him. On their journey it was revealed that Finn's father was Ar Elon, once High King of the land. But the old king had abandoned his

rule and, in disgrace, gone into hiding. Convinced of
his destiny, Finn decided to claim the kingship. Before
he could reach his father's court at Ormkill he was
taken aboard a ghost ship and swept away out of the
world. Finn passed a year among the dead. When at
last he returned, he went to his father's hall intending
to announce his birthright and claim the rule. There
he performed marvels. To many he seemed the very
image of the vanished king. Nonetheless, he was not
believed. Even his mother, who had come to the hall,
would not acknowledge him. Plotting with Thigg, Ar
Elon's steward, she tricked Finn into accepting a test of
his claim: he must scale the sacred mound on the island
of Tinkern and battle the witch who waited there. No
man would go with him. Even Tabak, seemingly, left
him.

Finn journeyed alone to Tinkern. There he met a girl
hiding in an oak; and, not knowing she was the child
Tabak had taken, he slept with her. She was Géar, his
own sister; and she, thinking he was Tabak and seeking
to preserve his life, murdered the witch in his place.
Neither knew the fault. But from the first Yllvere had
planned it. Now her children would have a son, a
sealman like the great men of old, his wild blood
unmixed with the coarse blood of the little men who
lived on land. He would open the sea road and rule
once more the lands beneath the sea.

The first part closed on Hren, an island off the
western coast of Finn's kingdom where the dead went
to begin their journey to the Other World. Here, Ar
Elon, his huge shape swollen and ghastly from too
many years on the land, had taken himself to die. He
forced Finn to fight with him and, wanting death,
permitted himself to be slain. In dying his flesh passed
through many changes. New faces, one after another,
gathered on his skull, peered out and changed again. A
few, before the changes took them, Finn had known.
The last face, when death was done with it, was Tabak's.

I.
Tywy

1.

The light rose south of the island. The wind, nosing at the rim of the world, uncovered it like the brow of a skull the peat had buried. The grave, great weight of all my lands could not withhold it. Beyond meadow and moor, the blue wall of mountains, it pulled itself free. So stones in winter are thrust above ground; even so the sun rises.

"May your bones lie longer in the earth," I cried to the corpse of my father. Beneath the cairn of stones that kept him, my father held his tongue.

Along the great hill of the island the dying grasses trembled. Their dry heads, humbled by the wind, leaned toward the mainland and whispered. It had not changed. The grass withers; men die. Gray birds gather over the wood and look southward. Cold-eyed ghosts, their bleak lives snatched too soon, walk out once more onto the windy hills. In the emptiness of their hearts they remember the hail fires and laughter.

"May you stay dead!" I shouted. The gale took the curse and blew it back in my teeth. I did not need to look—the blood was still on the blade with which I had struck him.

Once he was High King, Ar Elon, the lord out of nowhere. From the marshes of the moon he had come to them, from the mists beyond Mhor—the god alone knew—perhaps fallen nine nights from a star. In the beginning there was no accounting. But though a stranger, soon enough he sat at the councils. From his chair he gave judgments, his chair that was so huge that all who came after to sit in his place seemed as children. It little mattered that his voice was stern; the land prospered under his hand; that much, in wonder, men said of him. Like a summer, sang the *filidh*, he had come among men.

But one summer, like any other, soon passes. Sea hair, both black and green, grew again from his shoulders. Thick webs reappeared between his blunt fingers. Too late they saw what he was—his dark flesh ugly in men's eyes, his foul breath smelling of fish. Too late the old men remembered. Once before, the sealmen had come to shore. Still wet from the western ocean, they had walked up on the beaches; naked, they had invaded the towns. There they had taken themselves wives from the lesser folk on the land. Their wise eyes were shining; they had crabs in their hair. But the women, it is said, their heads filled with old tales and longing, went with them eagerly.

One night the young men broke into my father's chamber. With axes they splintered the door at the back of the hall. For the shame of their manhood they meant to butcher him, to pull him panting from the white trembling arms of the girl. He had already gone. So, with no accounting, Ar Elon went from my mother's bed.

So in winter the rains beat down on the roofpeaks; the gale blows incessantly. Then one day the light, without notice, pours out of heaven; the sky, once sweet with disorder, is empty.

I examined the blood on my fingers. My hands would wash clean of his blood. The webs that one day would

stretch between knuckles I could cut away. Yet beneath
the knife I knew the blood would spurt again, his blood
that gave me life and shared my veins, his blood
splashing on my wrists and soaking my long arms. I
swore, feeling my heart beat hotly, like a stranger I had
shut within.

The bracken was trampled where we fought, the
merestone littered with matted hair and bone. A few
late flies had come out of the air and settled. Soon
enough death would have them. Without pity, even the
least of things is taken. How then, I thought, shall a
man be free of it?

Sadly I handled the sword that Géar, my sister, had
given me. The god knows she had not guessed the use I
had for it. Her skin was ivory, her hair in shadow as I
stood over her, as I drew on my cloak to cover my
nakedness. She knew not who I was. Seeing her, what
man would have told her?

I went down to the pool where I had slaughtered
him. Though I was weary, I saw to my wounds. The
dust I washed from my hair and the blood from my
arms. The wind waves lapped the bank. They came
without ceasing, cold as any of their immense gray
sisters in the sea. This did not seem strange to me.
When, before the first age, the ocean rolled back
from the land, this one fragment of itself was left
behind. Here through long ages its bright deep waters
lingered, fed of nothing but itself, immune to the
drying wind, unwarmed in summer. But though men
spoke of it, until I climbed the hill, its place had
been hidden.

I knelt at its hard margins, bent from my shoulders,
my good eye open. The water flooded over me. For a
time my pulse, which had been booming, slowed.
Beneath the wind the great soft quiet seeped into my
veins. I thought, If a man could but breathe this, would

he not forsake the land? So almost, I would myself and let my stewards, whatever their failings, whatever the loss of my own glory, rule in my place. But all at once my chest felt tight.

Gasping, I lay back on the ground. Ar Elon would have been less troubled. But he was ocean born. I had not his magic or his skill. Instead I took the horn flask I carried in my cloak, unstoppered it and dipped it in the pool. Whatever charm the water had to soothe my wounds I meant to take with me. I stood then looking out.

The island lay at the limit of the land, just off the coast. From that high place all the West was ocean. Once, across its vastness Ar Elon rode to shore. I would not look at it. To the east the headlands of my kingdom fell away, retreating league on league toward Ormkill and the hall that in the years which had followed my father raised with his thick hands. Whichever way I looked I found his memory. I strained my neck to watch the heavens. But even there the sun, grown huge, had scorched the sky. Behind it like a length of bloody hair it dragged the clouds, the harsh hills under them smeared red with gore. My wits were frayed and it may be that I ran.

Long after, I came down to the island's eastern side, the beach in front of me. Across the salt grass and the dunes I saw the walls and roofs of Tywy, my mother's holding. The ramparts that closed the yard were set with fires. Smoke poured from the rock. In pale old-ivory wraiths it wrapped the walls, rolled out in angry plumes along the shore. From the sea edge inland, north beyond the dike, it seemed the broad earth burned. But Tywy was at its heart. A hot breath raked my face. It blew upon my rage as wind on coals.

"By Dagda, Lord," I shouted, "what right have such men to their lives?"

In truth I hated them who kept the fires, not any one I knew but strangers, my mother's kin. The smoke they made lay heavy as a corpse upon the land. I wished them dead.

Because I had no curragh with which to cross the water, I fastened the sword to my belt and ran out on the lip of land. The grave black water fell on me. But if the sea were cold, I did not feel it. I leapt through the waves with beating arms. Around me I heard the hollow thunder of the sea. Softly, slapping at my sides, it sighed his name.

At every side the water streamed with sand. I pulled myself up once more upon the land I ruled, which was Ar Elon's before it passed to me. The water moaned. The tall waves, sliding back, hissed along the beach like his lost breath. Hearing them sob and gag among the stones, I lifted up my arms and screamed. Gray birds reeled above the land.

Out on the hills three men were walking. Hearing me, they turned aside. With awful sureness they lumbered through the gloom until the smoke curled back from them, I saw their splayed, enormous feet and their heads like barrels and knew I wished no more to look at them. Hair like marsh weeds clung to their skulls; they dragged their arms. At sight of them, my long face blanched with pain.

They did not turn aside. As they came they passed a branch of alder from one to the other reluctantly. The last to hold the branch, when he had come abreast of me, lifted his head and gazed at me beseechingly. A sound like wind on leaves came from his throat; his breath was cold.

"Lord," he said, "I know not who you are. But we are brothers. The Mughain, our foster mother, plucked us from the wood and set us here to guard the coast, for none of her own kin would do it. In truth, we do not much care for it ourselves. But, lord, we cannot let you pass."

I knew that tears were streaming down my face. I drew my sword.

The second gray man took the branch. The smoke behind him blotted out the land. Now it blew around his knees and shoulders and tangled in his hair.

"Though barely we have life ourselves," he said, "for the Mughain when she found us had but one breath to blow our souls to life, yet the land we guard was made for living men. Into this kingdom, lord, we may not let you come."

In my eye, the *filidh* say, was sorrow beyond telling. The third man saw it. Desolately he took the branch. He held it trembling.

"Lord," he said, "the Mughain's house is poor. Her cattle all are barren and every woman is with child. No man would have them as they are. Her beer is sour. Even the benches in her hall are rotted through. Lord, we pray you, go back to the sea. Among the living there is no welcome for the dead."

I meant to think of something else. But Ar Elon came into my mind. I saw his face as it was when life had left him, the flesh already cold, the flat eyes still. "I am the king of this land that you would keep me from," I cried.

"Ar Elon, lord," he whispered and fell down humbly to his knees. He did not know the fault. It was enough I knew it. My anger opened like a wound, poured out; and reason fled with it. Already I had raised my hand.

With one quick stroke I took the head. Dully it bounced among the stones. The second I gave no time to howl. Before he found his strength my sword cracked through his shoulder, rent the woody flesh and came out stainless in the air. He crumpled, a pool of water dripping from his side. The last man scrambled, ducked among the rocks and ran. I lunged for him and grabbed his hair. I threw back the shapeless head so that the throat was bared. He saw the bright sword come at him. When it tore into his chest, he clutched the blade and wept. Again I thrust the metal in. He fell, his raw lips black with pain.

I turned to look elsewhere, to clear my head, and saw at my back the first man, his neck a foaming stalk, the second, trailing one grim arm behind him, rise from their haunches. They stood upright, the sea in back of them. Unwearied, wailing as they came, they ran at me and caught me in their arms, pulled at my legs and gouged my eye. Once more I brought my sword against a skull, high and upward from the shoulders. With ease I flicked it from its neck. But when I stepped too near the head, it set its teeth, undaunted, in my heel.

From one hour to the next I kept at that work. Their blunt black fingers snapped; before my fury their chests split, their long arms opening to piny, resinous veins. But whatever I hacked and tore shook itself and twisted back to life. My nostrils quivered and my eye grew wild. Yet I gave myself to the madness willingly. Then like cordwood they were cut apart, fell into pieces; but on the ground they healed. Among the stones, inexplicably they gathered root and fingers, pulled up their black old heavy arms, mounted to their brown strong knees and stood. I flailed at them, but Death, though it had dispatched Ar Elon and would take me when it could, would not have them. Wherever I turned it seemed only that I drew more dreadfully within their grasp. At every step they blocked the way, massed tall in front of me. Overshadowed, I could no longer see the sky. And yet my anger raged.

Evening was near; a dull mist crossed the ground. Still we fought. But now, more surely, I saw the sorrow in their darkened eyes, eyes set like thick brown amber

in their mossy heads, a thatch of leaves and broken
twigs bent over them. A second time that day, now at
the close of it, my pain unspent, I raised a cry. Then for
one clear moment my sight, which had been sunk in
the gloom of carcasses and severed limbs, was lifted
over it.

On a hill outside the town I saw the women of Tywy
assembled, their hair unbraided, their garments dropped
about their feet. Their rosy breasts they lifted in their
palms. Out of the midst of the women one of middle
years walked down to me. Like the rest she was naked.
The copper hair that fell to her shoulders was streaked
with gray. Her own full breasts she had thrust out,
white in both her hands. She called out something.
Staring, I did not hear the words but turned aside,
confused, my anger withered.

I dropped my sword. Still the women murmured
fearfully. From their backs a company of men crept
forth with ropes. But I had shut my eye and did not see
them until I felt their panicked fingers on my arms.
Thick ropes crossed my shoulders, pulled up sharply
through my legs. I groaned and when they yanked the
line, I fell. The ground came up at me.

When I saw again, twisting my neck around, I looked
out on the broad dark plain that rimmed the town. As
far as I could see the land was one vast ruin of splintered
wood, the branches smashed and scattered, whole great
trees uprooted and strewn upon the ground.

I shifted and saw her copper hair as she stood over
me. She had raised a sheath so that her breasts were
covered. I saw the shrewdness in her proud gray eyes.
Her hand brought quiet. The people waited.

"From this time and forever this place is' holy," she
called out clearly. "For in' one day he cleared a grove
one league on every side. Nor has any man done such
work since our mothers' mothers embraced the seal-

lords here on this same shore. Then this wood was planted. Since then it stood. But in one day this new lord cut it down."

I meant to stand and answer; the words were in my mouth. Straining, I had crawled up to my knees. Though since the morning I had labored, I had not lost my strength. But when I found my legs, a sudden weariness sucked at my heart. I felt it rising to my head, glowing until the earth was all one whiteness and there was nothing I could do but close my eye.

Slow blood was weeping from my wounds. I tried to move but, stiffened after sleep, I found that I could barely lift my head. My shoulders knotted, I lay in the darkness, my broad back deep in a rug of skins someone had spread along the floor.

Below the grate the fire breathed fitfully; now mostly coals, it gave no light. I listened. As far as I could tell, the room was empty and the household slept. The guards, if any had been called to keep the watch, waited beyond the doors, careless or themselves asleep. My mind wandered. Grown restless, I felt the stillness more sharply than my wounds.

I was alone. Even when I left Morrigan, when I sought no man's company, it had been with Tabak riding at my back. Then, though all the rest of Bede deserted me, I gathered Ceorl and kept him. In time even Ffraw, despite his older loyalties and his fears, came into my service. Their rough hands they gave in friendship as much as fealty. Now I had neither. In Ormkill, across the land, they shared the king's chair in my place, so far away it seemed no use to me. A king needs his companions by him; they give him balance and, if it comes to that, there is always someone there to bind his wounds.

I bit my lip and thought. The pink coals blackened. Through the louver in the roof a single dazzling star peered down at me.

It was some time before I noticed the carving on the wall. By then, though I could not distinguish faces, I saw clearly enough that they were figures of women, slender but of a size and roundness that, if cold rock could breathe, they might have lived. With aching pain I moved my head.

They stood, as in a procession, posed along the wall. In their arms they carried baskets but in the hand of one there was a scythe. Each face was turned; the profile cut in deep relief. With my eye I followed where they looked. Set back in the farthest wall, the image of stone rising out of stone itself, I saw the ragged cliffs of Hren, tall above a thrashing sea. From that bleak shore I had come to Tywy, my mother's holding. Here where I was, among the women, she had lived before Urien, in the years that came, brought her as a bride north to Morrigan.

I thought, I am in a shrine. The thought rose blackly in my mind. I knew it was a holy place, that some women's rite was mirrored on the wall. Once more I tried to read the faces in the dark; but the carvers had put no thoughts into the stone. I moved my good eye over them. One shadow, rounder and taller by some inches than the rest, blinked. She turned her slender neck to look at me. I heard the warm sigh of her breath.

"My lord," she said, "are you at peace?"

I stared. It was all I could do to move my head. She waited. "Tell me who you are," I said.

She smiled back tolerantly. "I am the Mughain. They were my liegemen who brought you here."

I looked more closely at the dark to see what other shapes it hid.

She shook her head. "I sent them out. It was not fitting that you should find armed men when you woke. Nor was it safe. Myself, I took your sword."

She stood out from the wall. During her long watch it seemed the very dark had melted with her flesh; she shivered now to drive it off. Even then it clung to her—huge, opaque, stirring up behind her gown. Thickening and reaching out, it was like nothing else except the churning fumes that smothered Tywy. Through such smoke, her foster sons had come to me. Until that moment I had forgotten. But now I saw again the havoc on the shore, the terrible moving wood, the stark black-fingered arms, frenzied and grasping for my life.

"I saw no wood," I cried out suddenly. "Not at first, not at any rate from Hren nor even on the beach when I had crossed the strait."

The Mughain smiled. Her pale lips parted slyly. "This is the cause of it," she said. "We built our fires with wet green logs. And when we had no more of them, with the linen of our beds and at the last with the beds themselves, all soaked in brine. Had there been need of them, we would have burned the houses and the barns or, with all else lacking, the stout ships resting at our wharves. So the smoke we made lay heavy on the ground, rolled out into the wood and covered it. When you came to shore, you knew not what it was and in your anger battled with the trees. This we did so that you would spend your wrath before you came to us."

My brow had furrowed. Her strange sad gentleness puzzled me. I said, "Yet you did not stop at that but met me there with all your women, your robes undone, your garments at your feet."

As though reminded, she pulled her gown more tightly around her breasts. She said, "So enormous was your rage, though the wood was broken, that I saw your anger had not cooled. I called my women. Those whose shame was too great we held. The boldest stripped the others until, young and old, as the goddess made women, we stood in front of you."

I listened but it made me wonder. "Lady," I said, bewildered, "how was it that you knew my rage and set all this before me?"

"Be patient with us, lord," she said. "It is your peace we crave." Once more she shivered. Had it not been for the darkness I was certain I would have seen a patch of color flame her cheeks. Surely it was in her voice. "Once," she answered softly, "there was a man the like of you, taller than our men ever were, walking up alone out of the sea. . . ."

I knew the name but would not say it. I felt her watching.

"Woman," I cried out fiercely, "such men are dead!"

But already she had crossed the floor. I felt her round arms suddenly, warm against my neck. I dug my head between her breasts. My great hands raked her hair, pulled at it until she sighed. I knew it hurt her. Yet through the night, as a mother rocks a child, she held me gently as I wept.

2.

I did not hear the endless long winter roaring of the sea nor did the shock of morning sunlight awaken me. When, late in the afternoon, I stirred, I was alone. For some hours more I kept to that place. Outside the window the sky had turned a brownish black. Hail rattled the thatch. No one came. In time the storm drifted away to the south. I rose and looked out. The long vista of the beach was a dull, cold silver; the sea was still.

I knew little of maps, not in those years. I thought only, I am here at the sea edge; all that is land and east is mine. To this day that thought comes back to me. I gazed across the shadows lengthening on the floor. By then any stableboy in Ormkill knew better than I what I was heir to.

The wide pillared hall was empty of furnishings. The hangings had been taken from the walls, gone, they let me know soon enough, to feed the fires that had saved them from my wrath. I did not doubt that there were some whose thin old fingers had dyed the threads nor that others there had stitched the winding colors to the cloth. They knew the loss but did not grumble. What fare they had they put in front of me. The Mughain had

15

filled my cup herself. It lay neglected now where I had
pushed it, unmindful of courtesy, beyond my reach.
Her proud mouth straightened.

"No," I answered stubbornly. "Fifteen winters she
kept him by her, tethered at her door, bound there like
any of her hounds—no more than that. Surely not a
king, not even a man, just a brachlet that did her
bidding." I looked around. "Yet can any tell me that in
all that time she had not guessed?"

The Mughain's chair was set up on a dais at the far
end of the house, beyond the hearth. Her mouth was
pinched. Sometimes, it seemed, she found it hard to
look at me. Once more her face, uncomprehending,
drew taut beneath her brows. The lame hag, Cerridwen,
stood at her back. She mumbled to herself or to the
Mughain. Strands of her iron-gray hair lay wet against
her mouth; her old woman's arms were blackened from
the fires. At their feet, holding the Mughain's footstool,
a young girl lifted her pretty head. Her yellow hair fell
forward. Puzzled, she shook it back.

"The seal-lords take whatever shape pleases them,"
she said impatiently.

The Mughain bent above the girl. She touched the
girl's long yellow hair and smoothed it. "He is young
yet for a king," she answered her.

But the girl stirred, unsatisfied. "He is tall as those
old lords. He swam the strait from Hren. Nor has any
man done that." Her look grew thoughtful. "It must be
that a man learns something being dead."

Cerridwen laughed. "Child," she said, "he is all the
younger for it then. For how can any man find life again
except as a babe?"

So for some minutes the talk went swiftly back and
forth, ignoring me. Listening, I felt my anger drive
within my veins. "I was not dead!" I shouted.

In the back of the hall the men of the holding, not

wanted at the hearth, gave up their muttering. One or
two were fussing with their arms. I heard the metal slip
out from the sheaths, the buckles rattling. Among the
Kell the women keep the mysteries and the rule. But
even to those without authority some truths are never
welcome. The Mughain saw it. Her bold eyes slapped a
warning on the faces of her kin.

"Of my own will I brought him to my house," she
told them sharply.

But a man had risen from his bench. He got up
slowly, letting all who cared to watch him see the knife
that he was dragging from his belt. Still, he knew what
he did. Beads of sweat had broken out on his old brow.
"Lady," he said to her, "we are not children that you
can disregard us."

The Mughain cast him an evil look but it did not
dissuade him.

"Myself," he said, "when Mabon died, my sister's
son, I laid him in the coracle. I rigged the sail myself
and pushed the small boat into the sea. Then swiftly as
a tern it sped away to Hren. Nor was it long before its
ribs lay broken on the rocks. So Duinn gathered what
was his." The man looked down. "These nine years I
have mourned the boy. Yet I am not a fool. If I saw him
now, even if he cried to me, I would not rush to take
the rotted flesh back in my arms." He glanced at the
Mughain, then at his brothers. "Let the dead stay
dead," he added loudly. His old hands were trembling.

I ground my teeth. "There was a man I left there. He
was dead. But as I am I came away."

From the dais Cerridwen grinned. "What does a man
know?" she asked the air above her head. She waited
until some shape that seemed to have gathered there
had gone. When at last she found my face, she grunted
softly. "Three deaths you shall have, my lord," she said.
Her eyes, watching me, grew hard with cunning. "A

day is coming when you will be given to the fire. But that is not enough. Another day is coming, worse than the other, when the sea that cradled you will suck out your last breath. Then all the waters of the earth will fall on you." She stood upright, no longer leaning against the queen's chair. The blood had pushed up into her white face. "So much will come," she whispered darkly, "as surely as you are born of woman. But the sword that waited from your birth to strike at you has done its work."

If she had more to say, I did not care to listen. So I laughed. "Is this the best wisdom of the Kell?" I asked. "Is this a corpse you see in front of you?" It was to Cerridwen I had spoken. The Mughain answered. Her face was gentle, amusement bright in her eyes.

"Has any man, even a king, brought one life from the womb?" She shook her head to show that this was foolishness. The women smiled. "How then can any man know what is taken when life vanishes?" Her lips, turning at their edges, smiled. A woman's smile. "You are not different. What you left on Hren you will not have again."

I stood rigid, my every muscle fixed on her. So it was I did not hear the quick hard scrape of boots along the floor. The knife, unlooked for, sank into the thickness of my back. I swung around. The man, his face twisted, had stumbled to his knees.

Clumsily I groped for the handle of the blade. Without thinking I found the grip and pulled it out. The bright cold metal glittered of itself, dry, unbloodied, as though the knife had been driven into sand.

Cerridwen stamped her small lame feet. "That death," she cried, "you have had already. Twice you cannot die of it." I turned away.

The men of the holding had scrambled back against the doors. Fear sucking at their throats, they made no

sound. But the Mughain had lifted her white arms and
screamed at them. All watched her. Only the girl at her
feet had turned to stare at me. Her thin breasts rose
and fell beneath her gown. If she had meant to speak,
there was no need of it. Her heart was shining in her
eyes.

The next morning the man was taken to the yard.
There, after they had strapped his legs, they strung him
headlong from a post; but it was the women, standing
back a score of paces, who cast the spears. He was not
young. His hair was grizzled, his beard hoary and
untrimmed. What little strength he held to left him
quickly and he died. They left him hanging for the
birds—a sign to the men of the holding—but no birds
came. When, late in the day, the clouds massed above
the land, they cut him down. Sadly, his brothers bore
him to the shore. Huddled over him, muttering to
themselves, they laid him in the boat. For a time I
watched them. Out of the southeast a stiff breeze
prowled the coast; still I do not know whether it carried
him across to Hren. Long before he would have reached
the rocks, I walked away.

South of the island the headlands tumbled back,
fallen into mounds of starved brown grass, mussel shells
and stone. Here through detritus and broken hills the
river from which the holding drew its name had chiseled a deep channel in the rock. Gathered from the
scarps and scarred, steep shoulders of the nearby peaks,
its current never slid through low soft bottomlands but
rushed with ceaseless fury toward the gulf. No desolate
islands stood in the river's path. Each spring the wharves
that lined the banks were washed away; the men rebuilt
them wearily, with curses, I thought, as much as tim-
ber. But I did not know this then and only saw how the
piers were dragged out on the beach.

Brooding I went along the bank. In the brisk wind the ships were tugging at their lines. I saw how small they were; only one had more than a single mast. I did not wonder that Pendyved had laughed at the men of Tywy. Their small ships never sailed beyond the sight of land. Their service, had the Mughain offered it, would have proved of no great worth. The rivermen of Abereth and Elderwyn, knowing little, would have known as much about deep water. They at least were accustomed to having kings over them and would have followed me more readily. But I put the thought away. From where I was, even hell, I knew, was closer at hand than Abereth.

As I walked on and had gone beyond a spur of land where the shore was hidden, cut off by the hills, I saw the girl who had held the Mughain's footstool. She was sitting high up on a boulder, her knees drawn up, and looking down at me. Though against the cold she had wrapped a worn brown shawl about her shoulders, the rag did not keep her from trembling. Her gray eyes flickered, shifting as though uncertain whether I would stop and speak with her. She need not have been troubled; I had had enough of my own company.

I climbed up among the boulders, out onto the bare rock where she sat like a gannet. "Why do you wait here?" I asked. "The Kell are gathered on the beach to watch Lord Duinn take back the dead." But her thoughts like burrs had stuck to something else. Her chin lifted.

"There will be another," she said soberly. "And if he cannot drive you from the hall, another after him. I know them, lord. They will not tire of it."

She watched me silently. In her nearness I felt a deep uneasy strength, slighter, I thought, than the Mughain's but real nonetheless and, in a way, more disturbing. Something dragged at my memory, my skin prickled and, though I did not know what to make of it, at first I did not answer.

She was no longer quite a child, yet her skin was smooth and white as beach stones, in places nearly transparent. The fine small veins were blue as bruises underneath. Her brows, yellow like her hair, had knitted together. But when I did not rise to go, she smiled.

"I am their king," I said. "In time, perhaps, they will learn to swear to me." She heard me out but answered proudly.

"Here the Mughain rules as her mother's sister ruled before." Slowly she let her gaze run over me. "As I shall rule when she is dead."

I was surprised but mastered it. "May you have a strong hand then," I said not unkindly, knowing it made no difference, that whatever their custom I was king. "And more luck," I added, "than I have had."

"It was never luck the seal-lords had," she said, "but the great old power forged beneath the sea." Her eyes were fixed on me with quiet certainty. "You cannot hide it. We were not sleeping when you cleared the wood."

My patience went. "Some were sleeping," I said, "or else gone off somewhere sharpening their knives." With cold anger I took hold of her arms. "What power is it that no men fear?" I asked, "that cannot keep even old men from meaning harm?"

She murmured thickly and looked away. "You cannot rule what is not yours," she said.

Whose she thought, it was plain enough. But then, I thought, she is the Mughain's; it is best she deal with it. I let my breath go out of me. She dropped her head.

"And what is mine?" I asked her finally. The color mounted in her face. Still, she did not need to think.

"The land that is not land."

I laughed. "So you would have me king of whales and fishes?"

Her face, unprepared, seemed honestly surprised. "Is that not the world's first kingdom? Cerridwen says it is, the first and perhaps the last that there will be. No little thing. More certainty than the few poor acres of stone the women hold at Tywy."

It may be that I saw the truth in that. I said, "But I have never been there."

"Lord?"

"Not to the deepest halls," I said. "And all I know of them I have only heard the *filidh* whisper after wine."

Some thought of hers had deepened in her eyes. "Then you must go yourself and see." Her brows flickered upward. "You mean to go."

Perhaps it was a question. I was not listening. I felt my hands spread on the rock, its surface cold as the waste of water hills, felt it moving, cold and dark, endless beneath the shifting sky. Once more out of memory the vague insistent waves leapt against the shore of the island. In the blue, still shadows of the trees, Géar, my sister, lifted up for me the child that was still waiting to be born. I heard his cry. A strange, sweet urgency plucked at my thoughts. Almost I would go. But then I thought, when I saw the island, the harper manned the sails. In Tywy I had no crew nor, in truth, any man to do me service. The stone bit into my palm. Suddenly my heart grew bitter. I said, "Will eagles fly down from your hills to carry me?"

Her mouth, I saw, had crooked into a smile.

"We have seen the ship," she said triumphantly. "Three days before you came to us we saw it, riding the western ocean, shining in the darkness like a star." Her eyes were bright and held me. "By that, as of old, we knew a seal-lord had come again."

But I had had a stomach full of the awe these women felt because a man stood over them. I stiffened, facing her.

"You waited here for me," I said, to speak of something else, "knowing I would come."

She stopped. Her jaw dropped. "I saw the look you had when the women threw their spears," she said. "When you turned away, I saw the path you followed and I ran ahead."

"What do you want?"

"To look at you."

We stood. Uncertain of what should then be said, I left the rock and turned back toward the river. Along the way she kept close to me, within my shadow so that as we walked my left hand for a moment brushed her yellow hair. It was a moment before I found my voice.

"Forgive me," I said, "but I do not know your name."

"Yllvere," she answered simply.

No man is born hating the gods; in time it comes to him. But I was young and slow to learn. Hearing her, I smiled. "I had not thought that name was much in use among the Kell," I said. But the wind was cold; it blew between us. "My mother—" I began but the wind went on grumbling and I let it go. When we reached the river, she ran, not looking back.

The hall was set on high ground and reached by steps. None of the works of men is measureless; and as such things are counted this work was only passing old. Still, I doubted whether among the women there were any living who had watched these gray stones lifted into place, surf stones and channel boulders hauled out slippery from the bay in summer, then strapped to sledges for winter cartage up the snow-smoothed hills. Little had been quarried on the land. The masons wanted searock. In places a delicate crust of bleached white shells still patched the stone; on others, vague impressions skittered mysteriously as though webbed small feet or fins had somehow briefly touched there and gone. In all, nine towers, like bluffs above high water, held the walls. Three jutted black and bare along the northern face; another three, their rough sides hidden by creeping stems and leafless ivy, rose from the cart road in the south. The last, as beautiful as they were precarious, coiled with their outer stairs about the threshold up to uneasy heights. I gawked at them.

It must be that the Kell thought they had built grandly—perhaps a seal-lord's keep, the memory of something once glimpsed shining undersea. But for all its splendor, the work was crude, the rock porous and pitted with sea worms. It ill fitted a stormy coast. Two of the towers I saw plainly were already crumbling. Huge, sliding gaps had opened between the stones. Trusting to night whispers and sailors' mutterings, the Kell were not revered for their skill as masons. Still, it may be they did not see this as a failing. The women, at least, believing the old tales, had never looked for permanence upon the land.

I mounted the cracked stairs warily. The doors stood open. The wind, tugging at my cloak, swirled around my legs and went on before me. It almost seemed as if the pillars, groaning, edged apart. The wind rubbed by them. One of us, I thought, will one day bring this hall to ruin.

The hag Cerridwen waited by the door, soot in her hair, her arms still blackened from the fires. She looked up when I passed.

"Lord," she said, "it is time I bathed your wound."

But my mind was on the girl and I answered sharply, "You have said yourself it would not harm me."

"I have said you cannot die of it."

With her small hand she took hold of my sleeve and, leading me, she hobbled toward the hearth. A high oak table had been pulled before the fire; on its back a wide basin had been set. Two housewomen waited at the side, one with a white water crock, the other with a pile of fresh linen neatly folded in her arms. When I came near them, they curtsied but their eager faces never left off watching me. Without a word to either, Cerridwen took the crock.

"You will have to sit," she said to me, "or I shall never reach your back."

She looked over her own bent shoulder, then called out brusquely. Before the wall where the spears were kept two men were huddling by themselves. They shrank back hearing her. Yet after a moment, mulishly, they found a bench and brought it out. The scabbards hanging at their belts were empty. They did not speak but dragged the bench before the fire and went off quickly.

"It would seem," I said, "the Mughain no longer trusts her word to keep the peace."

Cerridwen's hair was thin as the trails of smoke that coiled from the fire. As always she was frowning. "What peace can there be among such men?" she said.

"I have not wronged them."

"It is enough they have to look at you."

My lips drew back. "I see no fault in being who I am."

She laughed and shook her head. "You have faults enough. Yet they have not seen them. When they stare at you, it is only their own smallness that fills their eyes." She laughed again grimly and poked at the cinders dying in the grate. "But once, my lord, It was only women's tales they lived with."

"And now?" I said.

"They see more clearly what they are not."

Such talk, I knew, gained nothing. I ignored her. But since the bench was low, there was no easy place to rest my legs. I pushed them out and, settling myself as well as I could, I pulled the longshirt up from my shoulders. Where the knife had entered the flesh was tender; the touch of the cloth inflamed it more. Cerridwen

saw me wince; but when she had filled the basin and
gathered a swath of linen in her hands, she gave no
thought to it and scoured the wound with all her might.
I bore it while I could but then cried out.

"Your years have taught you little skill," I snapped. "I
would rather take the wound again than have you heal
it."

She dropped the linen. "Yet it must be done," she
answered spitefully.

"Then find a maid with gentler hands."

She stepped back where she could watch me. Her
sour look gave way to something like a smile. "I shall
call her, lord," she said. Then swiftly, despite her limp,
she scurried off across the stones.

I waited with the housewomen. By then a dozen
more had swarmed into the hall, their white arms laden
with cups and trenchers. Red sides of meat were hauled
in to be hoisted onto racks above the fire. Stirring and
chattering, the women might have been a band of
soldiers, weighed down with spoil, home from wars.
But I had lingered by the hearth and they hung back,
uncertain, and began instead to whisper back and forth
among themselves. The two beside me hovered, waiting.

"What is the name," I asked, "of the girl Cerridwen
went for?"

"Which, my lord?" said the woman nearest me. For
something to do, she scratched her neck.

"The one," I said, "fairer than all the Mughain's
women, who held her footstool."

She turned indignantly. "Yllvere," she pouted but
added nothing. Indeed such a heavy silence fell on her
I almost doubted that she spoke. Still, I pressed her.

"And were there others?"

"Lord?"

"With that same name."

"Now?"

"At any time," I said and swore, "in all your memory, back twenty, thirty years."

She smoothed her own fair hair; her eyes were blank. "Lord," she said, "I would have been no more than a child."

"It is not," I said, "so large a holding." My voice was cold. It slighted her. I said, "You would remember."

Yet she would not and shook her head and glared at me.

"Once," I went on bitterly, "there was another child, here in this same holding, a girl with yellow hair. . . ."

She looked away.

Along the wall, where only now the lamps were being lit, a door pushed open. With strange relief I met her eyes. Her feet made no sound on the floor. She came quietly, nervously refastening the brooch that held her gown. Sensing her urgency, the housewoman stepped aside. The rest were quiet; but at the hearth the gray-lipped servant, not wanting to seem idle, gathered a load of wood and, muttering beneath her breath, tossed it at the coals.

The dry wood, long kept indoors, caught at once. A bank of flames roared red against the walls. Then all at once the faces of the women, that had looked pinched and drawn with winter, bloomed. They stirred and twittered; startled by the flames, one or two cried out. But Yllvere seemed to draw some strength from it. She looked unblinking at the coals. Her arms and throat took on their color; her flesh turned crimson until it seemed her heart, grown suddenly too large, would burst. She looked at me. High against my chest I might have lifted her.

"Child," I said, "what year is this?"

She did not answer. Her nearness burned. I shut it out.

I said, "Who rules in Ormkill?"

She looked perplexed. "Surely, lord," she said, "you know him. The *filidh* say yourself you named him steward, Thigg, your own man...."

I waited. So I have seen a man gored by an aurochs walk away. Only later his friends went after him and found him dead outside the wall, the flies already settling on his eyes. For a time she hesitated. Then, not knowing what was wrong, she took the linen. I felt her hands on me, fevered, awkward, slipping down. She was surprised when it offended me.

"Send the women back," I ordered.

Thoughtless of any shame, she protested. "It is near the time for serving, lord," she said. "Shortly the men will come and all the women."

But she saw my anger. Reluctantly she gave the word and one by one the women went. I saw then how she steadied herself, how despite her confusion and doubt, her quick gray eyes had fixed on me. Even so, we were alone before she took a breath. She shifted nearer, one hand resting lightly on my shoulder, ready to be snatched away. But with the other she found the wound and worked at it. It stung. When I swore, her fingers stiffened.

"Lord," she said, "I do not understand. Cerridwen said you asked for me."

In the fire-warmed air her hair clung damply to her neck. Straightening unhappily, she pulled it back. I grieved to look at her.

"It is not the wound," I said.

The small muscles of her throat moved soundlessly. "Just tell me what you want," she said when she found the words.

I shook my head.

A pang of sorrow caught her throat. "Lord," she murmured but her breath went out of her. I held her eyes.

"I do not understand," she said once more, her dry voice quiet, hurt. "I have watched you since you came," she said. "First when you walked out of the bay and later in this hall when Cerridwen spoke and then once more when we were talking by the river and you asked my name. All the while I tried to think just what you wanted. Each time I looked at you. But still, my lord, I do not know. How can I?" Her head moved jerkily. "Your face so changes when I look."

I knew the words. Reaching out, I touched her sadly, gently, on the corner of her mouth.

On Géar Finn, I thought, the first snow has already fallen. The nights grow long. Soon the boy, never meant for life, will be laid squalling in his mother's icy bed. By morning he would have been strangled. Remembering, though I had not seen it, for it was only servant's talk, I thought: Now it cannot be more than a few months longer—perhaps in the spring when the great rains stab the ground. Then Urien—not the man I knew, not even the man I remembered but Urien nonetheless—will ride down from his mountain, from the house and lands that Ar Elon had ceded him. It was six days' journey to the coast but at last, prancing and impatient, his war-horse would canter lightly across the sand. The sea air would be still and heavy. Ahead of him, out of the fog, he would see the nine uneven towers of Tywy, the women's holding. The horse, the servants had told me, was a gelding. But Urien, his hair still black, his beard like wet dark wool, was still a man.

Her lips were soft. Under my hand I felt them harden.

"Child," I said, "though at first I did not know you, you are the same."

The doors were bronze and fitted with iron. When the Mughain threw them back, they rang. The air

stirred back of her, fluttering the rich embroidery of her
winter gown. Her fine red-copper hair fell in a dishev-
eled mass about her shoulders. Away from the fire her
face was white. The cold still clung from her crossing
the outer yard. Seeing us, she stopped. I saw her
anger.

"Why have you sent the women out?" she cried.

Yllvere glared at her.

Let in once more to jar the pillars, the night wind
swept on by us and pounced upon the flames. The
sparks flew to the ceiling. But in the grate the fire
blazed red as women's blood, terrible and triumphant
as the open womb. Cerridwen had not been mistaken.
As far as the women saw, it was a corpse that stood in
front of them. I thought: she never once asked the
name of the man I killed. I clenched my teeth. The fire
ate at my memory as rust eats iron.

"Lady," I said to the Mughain, "tell me who you say I
am."

Her hard small eyes found no comfort in my face.
"Why do you play with me?" she asked suspiciously.
"From my first I welcomed you. Against the warning of
the men of my own house I brought you in, though in
your rage you would have slaughtered us."

The worm of smoke that covered Tywy woke in my
thoughts. White as death it reached out from the
holding. I said, "It was the fires I hated. Those who
made them, I wanted dead."

It made no sense to her. "But, lord," she said, "it was
the fires that saved us."

Yet I could look ahead as she could not. "Who is to
say? It may be death would have served them better."
My long shadow lay across her gown. Her head was
tilted back to look at me. A sudden flush had risen near
her eyes; it left her puzzled.

"Why," she asked, "should it seem strange to name you to yourself?"

I took her hand. I had known its touch when she was old. I said, "You have not answered." Because she was afraid, I drew her nearer.

Abruptly as a girl she smiled. If Yllvere stared at her, she did not notice.

"You are Ar Elon, lord," she whispered.

"Dear Vydd," I said to the Mughain, "it is only you who must bathe my wounds."

3.

In my old age I made a list of all I lost. In the Book of Gedd I made it, eighteen vellum pages, jeweled and painted. Whatever I had misplaced or abandoned I put there—the sword that too late Urien had given me, the head of Tabak bloodied and hidden beneath the stone on Hren, a girl's dark hair, spread on my thick shoulders like a fan. I was three years at the work; for I had my scribes, hunched above the pages as I bent over them, change all the great names into ornamented beasts and the lesser names into a wood. Now clawed and branched, the script, the *filidh* tell me, cannot be read. "You have not looked!" I shout at them. Behind their white old hands they smile at me. But when the winter comes and great storms howl outside the doors I take the huge book from the shelf and run my fingers across the straggling sentences, looping forward and back as though following the spine of a serpent. They are old men but I am older. They do not remember the years before their births.

"How do you know my name?" she insisted.

My mind turned on the question awkwardly. "In the vast halls undersea," I lied, knowing that Yllvere saw it.

32

"Among the great lords there," I said, uncaring, "I heard it whispered."

The Mughain took up the linen. When she had soaked it in the basin, she applied it gently to my back.

"Ho!" I cried. Startled, I clutched at my sides with pain.

Quickly I fumbled in my cloak. Out of a fold I lifted the flask that I had filled with the soothing waters I had taken from the mere on the island. The basin I tipped unceremoniously onto the floor. But before she spoke I had restored it and into the wide mouth I emptied the flask of what it held.

"There is little enough," I said, "yet once this brought me peace."

In the brittle silence the Mughain once more lifted her arm; but above the basin, gazing into it, she stopped. A stillness held her. Unmoving, she lingered; a faint luminescence reflected back into her eyes.

"I have ruled as it was given me," she said slowly. Her voice was flat, the words coming from far away. "Here among my women I kept where I was—year after year—but no king came to me. And yet I was never such a fool as to take to my bed a man of my own holding. I bore no sons. My foster sons I pulled like alders from the marsh. But even the stiff life I gave them you took back." She blinked. "Now once again I am childless."

She turned her head then, wearily, forcing it until I felt myself the reluctance of its turning. "Now a king has come," she said softly, "out of the wide ocean as it was promised. From the walls of my holding I watched him walk up on the shore. Taller he stood than other men; his dark hair was shining." Suddenly the sound of her own voice seemed to trouble her; something pulled at her throat, yet she would not stop the words. "I have ruled alone in Tywy," she said, "a queen and yet a woman like any other. And what a woman could do I did, even with the people watching. Though he smelled of battle and blood still covered his arms, when he came before me, I threw off my gown." She paused. "But the lord, I think, was not looking. Or if he watched, it was only to see how my small sister smiled at him."

I bent my head. It had been in my mind to go east toward Ormkill, to sit at last in the king's chair that was mine and give the law. But I knew then that the doors of my own land would be closed to me. If any lord was meant to stand before her it was still Ar Elon. "I have no business on the land," I said harshly, more to myself than to the women. On Hren, beyond the dark gate on the hill, where I had taken the life of him the women longed for, I had lost my way. I said, "To me it does not matter. Whoever rules or is born here is not my concern."

My aunt looked up. "Lord," she said, "I am not asking what you think. I have seen my gray hairs and I live with them."

"Then tell me plainly."

To my surprise, she laughed. "I do not know it plainly. If I did, there would be no need to speak of it." For a moment, familiar and unhurried, she held my eye.

"I shall have a son," she said quietly, "not of alder branches but of flesh. How can I tell you? Yet I have seen him standing over me in a place that I have never been, a place heavy with peat smoke and small light. It is hard to see and yet, if I reach out my hand, each pot and vessel is where I put it. On the fire a fine old kettle is boiling. I smell the broth."

I did not wish to think. "What would you have me answer?"

"If this is so."

I started. "How would I know?"

"It was yourself who poured it out," she said and tugged at me. "Come. Look into it before it fades."

But when I stood over the basin I saw only the clear water and the dark old metal shining underneath. I heard only the shifting of her gown and thought, It is nothing. But all at once the water blurred, grew fathomless. The smoke that poured from the basin, which all of a sudden was everywhere, engulfed me. I battled it vainly. Angered, I waded into it and bumped my head.

Thick stalks and herbs, mountain flowers, dry and brittle, gathered in bunches, hung low from the rafters. I hunched my shoulders. Cramped beneath the ceiling, I stood as best I could, as I had once before when I was a boy and had no name of my own that men would listen to. I squinted but there was no need of it. Well enough I knew the hut and the old woman, thin as the stick with which she poked the fire. Her face was a nest of wrinkles. Seeing me, she looked up. Without wonder or surprise, knowing that in time I would come to her, she smiled.

"Agravaine," she said, using her old name for me, "I am pleased."

Out of the curling smoke, just above the table, a vaporous wing unfolded with a crack. The crow's black eyes stared back at me. My head throbbing, I turned away.

In the basin the water shimmered. Rag ends of smoke drifted through the hall. Forgetting where I was, I had stumbled. Had Vydd not held me I would have walked into the fire.

"Lord?" she asked, afraid.

Despite the pain in my skull I made myself look at her, Vydd, my mother's sister, to whom I owed and would owe wonder and longing, the gifts not given in my begetting. In the years that were already gone but

were yet to come she sat and would sit beside me by
the fire in her poor hut on the mountain. There, though
I was a child and impatient, she told and would tell me
tales of my birth. In that I might have been a son to
her. Almost I would have told her, but the wind blew
through the doors of the holding—the bitter wind from
Hren. I felt its damp breath on my shoulders and
shivered. In the shape of my palms I felt the cold stone
of that place where, amazed and desperate, I had
crawled from the cyclic and uncounted waves, out of
the waste of ocean where the long years rolled without
turning. I thought, Whatever happens is not finished.
Like serpents our lives turn back upon themselves.

"Lady," I lied to her, "I do not know the mysteries of
birth. Yourself you have said it. Such matters are for
women." Grimly I sat at the table, then after a moment
I reached for the basin, tipping it sideways, draining
the queer bright water back into the flask.

"Lord," she said helplessly. One last time she reached
out to touch my shoulder, to hold it. The fire gleamed
in the gray and copper of her hair, on the small weary
lines of her face.

She said, "I have no skill, it seems, in greeting kings.
But as I could I welcomed you." She went then without
another word, out through the doors of the holding, her
gown drifting behind her, to summon the women.

Yllvere watched me. She heard the slow indrawing of
my breath.

"What have you hid from her?" she said.

*It was my shape you saw, I thought, that first you
remembered when Ar Elon came to you. So you went
and will go to him, gladly, not knowing the fault,
thinking how once you had met in the years that are
already gone but not faded, thinking, Already I have
bathed his wounds.*

I did not answer. At my back, grumbling among themselves, the men of the holding came into the hall.

There was no peace that night but after the death of the man there was quiet. The men found their places somberly and sat staring at their hands or plucking at their boots. The housewomen, uncertain why they had been ordered out and then as quickly brought back again, hurried through their work with a discontented stillness but with care. Straightaway the meat was put onto the racks and lifted over the fires. But if their hands were busy, their faces were drawn. I saw how they watched me, pausing when they thought I was not looking. A few were pretty, but with the onset of winter their sun-whitened hair had begun to darken. Against drabness they had smeared goose fat into their pallid flesh until it shone. Their braids, freshly plaited, hung over gowns that had been left all morning to air in the yard. As they jostled back and forth their arm-rings glittered. But I asked nothing of them and they went on with their labors sullenly.

By the time the trenchers had been brought out and the bread loaded onto the table the wind had died. The smoke holes were not drawing; a blue haze fell like webs from the ceiling. The men coughed and, remembering the dead, ate sparingly. I could not see into their faces, but I knew the shame in them and did not fault it. All men, seeing death, must die a little. Still the man was none of mine and after the second keg had been broached, I pulled my chair aside. The unfriendliness of the lower hall, where at last the men had begun to stir at their cups, had not improved; I saw nothing to be gained in waiting for the beer to warm them. Already some tongues were loosening.

As I went by one of the benches a man stood up unsteadily. I saw him swallow.

"Every fool thing we have done," he said.

I looked at him blankly.

"Every fool thing they have told us," he said bitterly.

The Mughain had risen but I laughed and pushed on by him.

The light from the hall stabbed in yellow spikes through the shutters. Gleaming, it poked into the yard. But under the wall, beneath the low-sweeping eaves, the darkness closed in upon itself. Groping, I caught my boot on the edge of a flagstone and stumbled. Even at that, it was a relief to get out into the air. Behind me in the hall someone shouted. The sound seemed far away.

The yard sloped to the south, turned crookedly along a lane that wandered through a cluster of squalid sheds, then lost itself utterly among the byres and forges, the lesser outbuildings of the holding. Somewhere ahead of me I could smell horses and the damp strong odor of winter hay. To the left, I thought, was the shrine where I had slept after I had cleared the wood. I remembered the rug of skins that had covered me and hoped no one had gone off with it. In truth, I longed for sleep. I went, following my memory, under a low arch and up a short run of stairs until I came before a rough door in the rock. But when I gave a shove to it, I found it bolted.

In the nearer darkness a curlew shrilled. The air, I noticed, was heavy with the scent of kelp. I could hear the water and knew I had gone too far. Bewildered, I turned back once more, trudging up the slope and counting the houses. That is the wellshed, I thought, for I had passed it in the morning. But when I had come up nearer to it and mounted the blunt worn steps, I found that it was not. For a moment I stood puzzled, looking out into the yard. Too tired to think, I leaned my shoulder heavily against the door. With a groan the thick boards pushed inward, spilling me into a narrow room.

A single lantern swung from a wallspike, dangerously, rocking back and forth. Its light was poor, but after the darkness I had to shade my eye. I blinked. At the center of the room, her head uncovered and powdered with the dust of grain, Cerridwen was working a quern. Her thin fingers were wrapped about the shaft that moved the upper stone. Gritting her teeth, she pulled at it. The floor stone growled, sending a shiver through the walls.

"Latch the door," she said, not looking up, "or they will find you."

Before I thought, I had put my hand to the metal.

She snorted gently. "It is a wise man," she whispered, "who, uncomplaining, does a woman's bidding."

"I did not leave the hall to hide from them."

She did not answer. Instead, her frail hands closed more tightly on the shaft. Grunting, she swung the stone. The thick floor rumbled; the dust flew up and rimed her hair. Something tugged at me, making me dizzy. For what seemed a long while she kept at it, but at last, out of breath, she stopped. Then for the first time, her meager chest heaving, she looked up. "Now open the door," she said.

"You bade me close it." Yet, unthinking, stiffly, I found I had put my hand to the latch. The door squealed open. But when I stared out, my eye grew wide.

The dark long walls and the towers had somehow slid over to the left. The mountain behind the hall was fixed and still, the same bright stars frozen over it. Everything was as it should have been except the houses, sheds and barns, and even the flagged yard under them, had seemed to turn like pieces on a potter's wheel. In all things they were unchanged and perfect, only they had come to rest facing another way. Doubting, I shook my head.

"How have you done this? Why?"

Her eyes looked off. "To save your life," she said, and pointed.

Across the yard, where before I had missed it, I saw the shrine. On the seaward side, crawling along its length, two men scraped low against the ground. Between them they dragged a heavy bar. Making the steps, they straightened, hefting the bar up after them. Hurriedly they set it in the doormounts. Then as one stood back, the other, wielding a hammer, beat the ringing metal into place.

At once, as though the sound had been a signal, the doors of the holding burst open. A stream of men came blundering from the hall. The smoking torches in their hands waved drunkenly. Their short arms and small red faces jerking in and out of light, they ran across the yard. Swarming among the sheds and shouting, they bunched up at last before the dark walls. There, they crawled up on each other's backs, scrambling nearer the roof. The flames on the torchheads, unsteady in their hands, paused and wobbled. Then someone shouted, once clearly above the rest. The men who had got into the eaves tossed up the brands.

The walls were stone, but the roof was thatch, dry straw and wattle. Small gulping fires caught at the edges. But quickly, finding the seams of pitch, they ran a dozen courses toward the peak, flaring until, just at the summit, the fires raised one glowing head, like a yellow crown, golden, shining on the night's black shoulders. The burning seared the air. Heat pounding their faces, the men fell back. Within the hiss of flames a roofbeam moaned, cracked inward suddenly and fell crashing with a roar. About the burning shell of the building the small men cheered.

But I was quiet. It was my death that made them howl.

"Very well," Cerridwen said. "You have seen it. Now close the door."

Turning, I saw her face, red, like her gown, in the light of the burning. Her fingers loosened, then stretched out again about the shaft. I closed the door.

"Cerridwen," I began.

"Hush," she whispered and took a firmer hold of the shaft. A deep unending pulse rumbled through the floor, knocking the loose stones from the wall. The chamber held for a moment, then, groaning, pulled beyond its strength, it twisted. I waited for the blow. But nothing touched me, only a wave of blackness dark against my eye. Then as suddenly something clicked, slipped softly into place and stopped. The walls that had seemed to tremble found their old hard shapes again. I stared. Cerridwen dropped her hands.

"It is done," she said wearily. "You have your life. Though it is little wonder the men at our holding hate you. Yet the debt we owed is paid."

I felt the muscles in my jaw grow hard. I had bargained enough with women. "There is nothing owed," I said.

She raised her head. "Too well we loved you, lord." She almost smiled. "More than our husbands, loved when we should have hated you, you with your stench of blackness, the salt still in your hair. More than our own fair sons we loved you. That is fault enough."

Her gray loose hair had drifted across her face. She pushed it back. So Yllvere might have done. So might any of my sisters.

"Still, I took away the death they planned," she said. Watching me, she sighed. "Yet you might have smiled on one of us. If not out of love at least from pity. Here among my women you might have got a child."

I flinched. "It is done," I whispered. "On Tinkern through a woman's trickery I left my seed."

Her lips pulled tight. "That time has yet to come."

"It will?"

"I know it."

"And me?"

"Yes," she nodded wearily. Then sadly, "Yes."

"Not what your women think but who I am."

"Yes."

The flame of the lamp flickered on the dry lines of her face. She leaned forward, resting her thin arms on the quern. "But you are the one who came," she said, "the one we saw walking from the sea." She straightened, her gray eyes waiting, still. "How can it matter then whether you are Ar Elon or his heir?"

"To me it matters."

"No," she spat, angry all at once. As suddenly the life that was in her seemed to shrink and fade, the life that clings to flesh and marks it, man or woman, from the pale, uncaring earth. Only her eyes were left. Blank and empty as the winter sun, they watched me out of their ragged holes. "Here you might have ended it," she said, "cut short your branching lives and stilled your blood."

But I knew only my anger. "No," I cried, "You are no judge over me," and swore.

She made no answer. From beneath her cloak she drew a sword. Its deep-carved hilt shone with the warring images of men and birds. It was my own. She saw the deadly thing it was and winced when she gave it into my hand. "Take this plaything then," she said. "Now surely you will have need of it. For you are Duinn's now and none of mine."

My fingers closed on the bright hilt greedily. But it

was not for myself alone I took it. "Witch!" I cried. "It was a woman who first put this in my hand."

She drew a breath and I saw once more it was a woman breathing, tired and old, the strangeness gone from her. "Dear Finn," she murmured, "you were ever slow to learn." I would have answered, but sadly she hobbled to the door and opened it. One last time I saw how the house had turned and the darkness with it. The empty light of morning lay on the shore. The wind, nosing among the sheds and houses, blew over the threshold. In the roots of my hair and in the creases of my lips I felt it, grave and uneasy and tasting of salt.

So I fled my kingdom without one man to do me service, leaving the hut of Cerridwen, though the land she lived in was my own. They thought me dead. Still I did not follow the clear path down to the shore but prowled the brown lands and the fens by the river. There, I judged, I could not be seen, not from the hall nor higher up from the towers. No one gave chase. And yet I did not doubt there were some who picked through the stones, turning the smoking timbers for proof of my bones. The mired ground sucked at my boots. I listened. No shouts shook the air.

Gradually the bog gave way and I waded through water up to my knees. Even then the tide was going. In time I had worked my way into the cuts of streams, following the tide out until the water ran only at my ankles. On the banks small brown troops of crabs, all remnants and stragglers, the last of the season, moved through the grass. The birds were gone. The great birds never came ashore in winter. Solitary, far over the ocean, they lived and fed. The cold moon silvered their feathers. So they kept apart through the dark half of the year—watchful, unsleeping, far from their kind.

Had I been other than I was, I would have had a

troop of my own to keep me company. But another man, his cup well filled, resigned to the women's fire, would have had no need of them. Despite the bright air, the sharpness of morning, he would have stayed ashore. Better he would have been for it. It needed no witch to know the weather. The wind came ruffling out of the northwest. In a week there would be ice in the marshes and in another, on the hay fields, on the dunes, nests of snow bending and crippling the stalks of grass.

Out on the windy flats I looked over the water. The tide ebbed, draining the marsh. Yet beyond the land the sea was not made greater by its going. So the ocean will take me to itself, I thought—quietly, without notice, with only the cold and wind for company.

I paced the shore. In the cover of the grass I found an old curragh held to a sunken post with snarls of rope. My sword, I knew, would have made shorter work, but such use demeaned its worth. Slowly, with my fingers, I unplaited the knots. When I had done, I dragged the black hulk from its place and hauled it through acres of stinking mud down to the channel.

The craft was heavy, the old skins sodden, needing restretching and rubbing with wool grease. But I did not much care how well it would last in the sea. I wanted it only to carry me across the strait, then around to the far side of the island where my ship lay at mooring. Though I had done it once, I was now of no mind to swim the distance. To keep clear of the holding I had gone farther south and so more than doubled the length of water I would have to cross.

I stopped for a breath and looked seaward. The air was filled with the strident hissing of waves. As they crashed on the shore I counted them, and when I knew the lull would come, I pushed into the slack. The sea rose suddenly. A plume of water drenched my back.

Still I am away, I thought, though, in truth, I had yet to escape the land. The peat-black waves, muddied by the Tywy, thrummed on the leather sides. I could still smell the land, the scent of marsh grass, the weed smell of the shoals, the close, fetid stink of miles of mud.

Low in the water the curragh, despite the current, dragged. Without stirring, before I had put my back to the oar, for a moment the great sloping line of a wave lifted me. I looked up. High on the bluff, above the nest-strewn crevices and empty ledges in the rock, I saw a pair of figures running, racing ahead until the land ended and they stood at the edge, their long hair streaming back. A third dim figure limped up behind. Then three together they stood, one no different from the others now, distant, no more than shadows. I heard a cry. Scattered by the gale, only a thin sound lingered. Like the sad, sweet crying of birds it drifted over the strait.

So it was that I abandoned them and not only the lands and women but all that was mine: the first spring calving of the aurochs; the ripe, swollen fruit of the trees; even the salmon, red as oakwood, unwearied, climbing the falls—mine by right whether bear or man caught him. I took only the sword that Cerridwen gave back. So the sea would not rust it, I had wrapped it in my cloak.

II.
Tech Duinn

4.

This only I set down, myself, in my own hand. I see the letters, slight and cramped. I have to squint to look at them.

Even Grieve, who taught me, whose kindness held out longest, would have laughed to see this thin scraping of my outsized hands. Bears, she would have said, if taught their letters, must write like bears. In massive strokes, she would have said—like the bloody swiping of their paws. Had they known of it, my scribes would have nodded solemnly. But kings, they would have added—knowing their place and knowing mine—kings ought never to write at all.

Indeed these books are scribework, taken down as I paced the hall, my robe neglected, forgetful even of the winter and the cold, while they, wrapped and bundled, pressed near the fire and, listening, made their bold marks dutifully or because I fed them. More likely that. For who in this fool's age would give work to scholars if the king will not?

But this they did not do.

The rest I knew. After I had rehearsed the words, I spoke and they wrote down. But when I had told them how I took the curragh and left the land, how the wailing women watched me go, I sat down glumly.

They waited, thinking, He is weary. Only let him call for wine and he will start again. Or, because I had kept them long in the house, He is only thinking. Some cold thought out of his memory, breathing freshly upon him, has made him quiet. Only wait and he will find the words. So they waited, alert and grave. So they would have waited—thinking, It is only a moment—until morning.

I sent them out.

The young men went eagerly, went to relieve themselves in the yard, went unconcerned to climb into the lofts, to find, if they looked for it, the uncritical warmth of a girl. Only the old men lingered. They stood in the cold and dark. They made much of watching the wood smoke, the last sparks of the coals, thinking because they had no women who wanted them, had as I had only sleep in front of them, that I would call them back, thinking, It is only some old man's secret, some matter of love or pride he will not let the young men hear.

I banged the floor with my stick until they went.

It was not, I am certain, forgetfulness. The thoughts of some men molder, grow soft as age takes hold of them. But even now I can recall a bent face by the loom, a white arm lifted, the smell of wool . . . even fifty years after, a smile I saw just once and never saw again. It was not shame. That I had groped and fondled my own sister, had mated her, by now men knew. They knew its issue. How can a war be hid from those who fought it? For myself, I had made too many corpses to suppose I might bind the wounds of living men with lies. It was not pride. As I knew the tale I told it. But of the leaving of Tywy, except for the wailing of the women, I have no memory. But neither, the god knows, have I forgotten anything.

* * *

It snowed, the white storm pouring silently out of a darkened sky, the close sky lowering until the space between the waves and heaven was no more than the length of the second mast. The foremast, from the sprit onward, belonged already to the upper world. Life narrowed. Pressed between sea and air, the far-off roar of breakers echoed dimly like faint sounds heard in caves.

Fearful of the rocks, I had come on deck. The air was cold. Snow, swirling over the bow, danced in the rigging like damp white moths. Except for the distant surf, the sea was calm. The darkness sucked my heart.

It was that I remember—before all other things— awakening without any sense of sleep to a world some- how diminished, moving cramped against a smallness made more terrible because it hovered just out of reach.

I could not see the land ahead, but through the quiet storm I heard it, the long waves rolling onto the rocks. I broke the ice and, when I had freed the line, cast out the anchor. I felt it drag, groping, the bottom near. After one false catch, it held. Swung back from its ruin, as though begrudging safety, the great ship groaned.

The woman will not hear of it. "It is twelve days' journey out from Hren to far Tech Duinn," she inter- rupts. "No less than that. You who had no skill with ships, nor men to follow you or work the sails, no provisions even for a man alone, how did you live to see that place?" She does not smile.

Her father, before I made a lord of him, was a linen merchant down in Harl. A steady, strapping ugly man with bright corn whiskers, he was good company and in my court or on the field my surest judge of men. Sadly, he had no head for figures. From the day I met him until I put a stop to it, his daughter, knowing his worth as she knew her own, kept his ledgers and accounts.

The hall is quiet. She holds my eye, weighing my look as I stare back at her. To this day she will have me to the penny.

"Who marked the distance then?" I growled at her.

"Husband," she answers quietly, "it was Meth Clêr, your own shipmaster."

I frown. "He is a brave man and I find no fault in him. Yet, lady, he himself never sailed from Hren."

Her small white hands are folded in her lap. She has no need to lift them now. Yet in her father's house, where we had been left alone the night I told her I would have her as my queen, she had hurled herself down and clasped my knees. Then, until I took an oath I meant it, she had not let me go. Now she looks past me, across the hall.

"Has any man?" she asks.

I summon a girl to fill my cup.

"No man," I answer evenly, "only a king."

All day beneath the planking I sat brooding, walled by the ship's ribs, keeping what warmth I could with a small round pot of coals. Even in the thickening cold, when numbness invades the limbs and reason fades, there is a kind of peace. I slept. It was evening once again when I awoke. The storm was gone.

I hugged my shoulders and, jogging on my toes to bring back feeling, climbed upon the deck. I looked out through the linked ropes in the bow. A gritty light still slanted through the clouds. Low and squalling, they rolled on westward. I gave no thought to them. A huge white island reared up on my left. Southward the coast was steep, piled high with snow-patched stone and hanging crags. But northward the tall peaks halted, leaving abandoned towers in the rock as though here where air and water met, the elements, seeking once to fashion a common measure of their might, had some-

how gone beyond their strengths and let it be, not
overthrown or ruined, but just unfinished. The desolate, uneven dunes swept again into the sea. The shore
was rubble. Pounded by the surf, the cold stones rang.

I knew nothing of this island. But it had no harbors,
no place to land. No herring boats, whirled out by
gales, their crews half-starved, had thought it safe to try
its beaches. No men at least had come wide-eyed back
with tales of it. Better a slow death tightening belts
than certain slaughter on the rocks. Pushing on, they
either starved or drowned. And yet I hungered.

With no better claim on me, I kept my vigil and
thought of cormorants and gulls and snares to catch
them. I remembered, oddly, how when I was a child,
out in the pantry Grieve had left, against ill-luck,
offerings of milk for elves. Great saucers filled to the
rim they were. For a quarter-hour, until the last light
drowned, I thought of little else.

The ship, unminded—pulled at its anchor by the
tide—drifted shoreward in the dark. It scissored back
and forth before the land. Too late I felt it slide. Across
the outer bar the black sea rolled and staggered on the
stones.

There was no chance to wait for morning. The sunrise would have found me pinned beneath the mast or
slivered through with twisted wood. The keel struck
ground. An arm of water slashed across the deck, shook
loose the planking and hooked me at the knees. With
no more time to think I leapt down from the rail, swung
for a moment from the ledge above the tumbling sea
and dropped. My head snapped back and water rushed
into my lungs. I gagged. Yet I did not seek the air but,
lulled by darkness, dreaded it. Far beneath the rushing
sheets of foam I closed my eye.

The Kell say each wave has its own soul. In truth, the
roar when long waves shake the beach, heard in the

darkness, will seem the cries of people in the sea. The hosts of drowned men call out in their sleep. Nor have I found fault with that. For when I moved within the galleries of the dark, borne down by black cold arms, the hair along my neck hard-laced with ice, I felt the wayward, longing sighs of other life. In the grinding undertone of stones, the hiss of sand along the shoals, I heard their guarded whispers and their screams.

Somewhere out ahead of me an avalanche of water jarred the world. So I would find my death, Cerridwen had said.

But in the darkness I remembered that I wanted air. Wildly, knowing that to live I must make the land, I stretched out my arms. My head was turned, my one eye open.

From underneath I saw the monstrous gray corpse rocking in the harsh waves over me. The uncurled, huge fingers spread; they reached down helplessly. I looked into the tangle of his hair. His sad, blank eyes were staring. Then, though the sea was full enough, I would have wept. But the hand was swift against my throat.

I seized the wrists. Flinching in the grip, I broke it. The arms had softened. The gray old flesh that he had molded by his will had weakened, changed. The sea itself was not the same, the mutinous dark waves that once had seemed to struggle with the sky fell silent. Lapsed back into foam, they lapped his sides. He did not speak. Yet the old fear welled in me. He cannot have my place, I thought. Nor would I ever let him wash to shore.

Reaching up, I grabbed his heels. With only a touch, like a bladder poked with a knife, he fell. His legs closed around and over me. I pulled him down.

On the cold sea floor I set him on a stone. As I had on Hren, I rolled up rocks to make his cairn. But when

I went to put the last stone down, to close his eyes, the head moved sadly on his neck. Already rotted, the face gave way and one last shape was roused up from his flesh. I stared and yet I did not need to look.

On Hren in my anger I had not thought. But now, remembering, I saw how with his murder he had baited me. It was not his death I made. I never took his life; he gave it freely, knowing it was not lost. Better than I knew myself, the women saw what thing I was. With my own hand I had piled the rocks on every side. On my own face, unbelieving, looking up, I had laid the stone.

Up from deep water the huge old sealman hauled himself into the air. His nostrils twitched. His dripping skin lay furrowed on his back; his hair was matted. As though uncertain, he tried the air. But when he felt it rush back biting to his lungs, he raked his snarled long graying beard and smiled. Curled under the light of stars, the waves grinned up at him. Only then, like a lord who had received his due, he turned to watch the land.

Tall crags, barred to him by walls of surf, loomed overhead. His deep eyes narrowed, studying each thick shadow in the rock, every star's thin glimmer on the ice. It was a cheerless place to come to land, he thought, and yet he knew a hundred other isles, each colder, each ringed about with vaster walls of surf. In the clearness of his memory, bright as dreams just out of sleep, the old lord named them to himself.

The Island of the Wind, he thought, for wind was first; the Island of the Shouting Wind, for that came next, and an island each for its four quarters; the six ice islands the six winds hardened out of foam; the Island of Virgins whom the gods made cold; the Island of Maidens who three times rebuff the men who come to them . . . and so he named them quietly, remembering. With each name he drew an icy breath until his cold flesh that never wanted warmth began to shiver and his blunt teeth chattered in his mouth. By then, swept free of clouds, the sky had become both high and deep. But his eyes, once clear, were rheumed with thought. Yet he could not name the land he saw.

Then I must go to it, he thought.

League-long waves had massed in rows beyond the shore. Unconcerned, he let them pull him from the edge. A mass of water thrust up slow and thick. At its swollen crest it rippled. Then all at once, tripped by the cutting rocks beneath, with a resounding roar it fell apart. The boiling rush rebounded from the beach. Fountains, spewing foam, shot up and battered him. The water caught him round the chest. Yet, hardly marking it, he moved against the surf as he had moved in battle against a crowd of men. His broad back took the blows. Row on row, the long black waves hurled down on him. He waded in.

A grizzled, burly man stood in his way. The waves swarmed over him, broke on the ledges of his shoulders. Yet he might have grown there like a stone, brown kelp clinging to his six long arms. His head was bare, his hair curled tightly to his scalp. The sealman saw his eyes. In the poor light of stars, they shone back brightly. He did not stir. Though he had left off his mail and had brought neither sword nor ax with him, by his bearing it was clear he meant no man to pass at either side.

"How are you here?" he shouted. In between the cataracts of surf, before the next wave fell, there was a silence and the sealman heard him.

"I have come upon a hundred isles," he answered back. But then he had to shout himself above the thunder and the drag of stones. "Nor," he bellowed, "has any man long stood in my way."

As though the other spoke to it, the next wave held. "Longer will I stand in front of you," he said and motioned at the land with one of several arms. "For here," he added, "no man who ever was has come."

The sealman looked at him, took the measure of the other's reach, assessed his quickness. He listened to his lagging breath. Then joyously the sealman straightened. "How should this shore be different from the rest?" he boasted. "On twelve islands I met the heralds on the shoals. Bold men they were, who did not leave their swords at home. Bold men, they met me bravely. Still the eels had bones to suck when I was done."

Another wave had left its place and fell. The sealman felt the whip of white surf, the cold weight of the sea as it poured over him. "Twelve times," he roared above the noise, "horsemen drove at me from stations in the rock. They were not clumsy. Carefully they aimed and hurled their spears. Yet their mares did not go hungry but had manflesh for fodder when evening came."

A flood of marbly foam engulfed his knees. The sealman felt it thrust between his legs but did not move. "Nor can it be otherwise with us," he said. "For I have never raised my arm against a man and missed my mark."

A great wave fell to ruin. The baffled water ran downhill against the sea. Then there was silence. He waited.

"Yet you are dead," the other said.

The sealman's mouth grew taut. For a breath's space he wavered, grew anxious. For a moment, distracted, he looked beyond the man. He saw the white worn winter hills, the grim gray stones along the beach. Over half-seen shapes the dust of snow had thickened. It seemed to him that he had never seen such lack of glory. "Has there ever been a more unwanted land?" he said.

The other nodded, "It is bleak work making mountains."

The sealman only gritted his teeth and swore. "You rant," he said, "and it is empty."

The other gave a sigh. He stretched his six brown-knuckled hands before him. The churning waves wrenched from their patterned fall. They melted into one black crest that, screaming, reared. Out of the awful cold and mist there came a woeful keening. Unyielding, the sealman pressed against the noise. Four hands reached out and took his thighs and bent his arms. Blunt fingers stabbed about his throat and squeezed.

The sealman gave a short, incredulous cough. The buzz of glowing sparks surprised him. His chest was tight. Never before had his cold lungs wanted breath. He was Ar Elon. Could he not dive whole days beneath the pounding seas, his thick hair weaving into darkness, down countless fathoms to the shining floor? Had he not raced with dolphins through strange deep halls, unhurried when even they, his brothers, rose for air? But now his fierce lungs ached for breath. He fought but could not free the arms that held him. Because he could not stand, he crawled, bewildered, sick with rage, and scraped a trough to hide among the stones.

Far off he heard the ocean's roar. But nearer, swollen up inside his ribs, a shapeless darkness turned like something in a sack. It wiggled. He did not weep. So it is only death, he thought, and felt, for an instant, as through a shell, a naked beak peck through his flesh.

A cold rain of spray fell on the rocks. From rents and smoking pools blasts of icy vapor blew into the air. I was tired, too tired and hurt to stand, and when I tried, I crumpled. The slow dark river of the tide, its fury broken, rolled gasping at my knees. There, sunk into crevices, diverted into rifts and faults, it hissed away among the broken slate and stones. I wished that it would carry me. I wanted only to lie down with it, to slide, uncaring, back into the sea.

"I will bear you," a voice spoke softly at my side. Thick arms covered with woolly hair embraced my shoulders; long arms crooked high around my chest. With easy strength they lifted me.

I squirmed but dared not meet his face. Four great arms shifted, found a better hold; another arm, unneeded, pointed ahead. My tired eyes followed, north, along a narrow valley cut back by a snaking river into the hills. At its far end, strangely clear in the distance, I saw an immense stone house raised up beyond a gate. It was shaped like a crofter's hut, save that it was higher and wider and had a great many windows. Its sprawling roof of heather thatch seemed broad enough to shelter not only the hall at Tywy but all its sheds and byres together. I looked back and then looked up again, amazed. Its doors stood open. The shifting light of fires poured out from it. My heart leapt and I clutched his hair.

"It is not far," he spoke up reassuringly. "Before morning I will have you there."

Then quickly, as though my weight were no more than a pack of wool, he left the beach and, mounting the stone, in a moment he was bounding along a rocky trail beneath the hills. Soon on either side tall cliffs rose up like towers. Their grim shadows lay across the track. He ran ahead.

We did not speak. On my left I heard the moan of water stumbling seaward under plates of ice. Though I could not see the river, now and then, a hundred elhws below, I caught a glint of silver; but then the night closed in once more; the cliffs grew higher and the wind blew cold.

Braced to his back, I felt his heavy shoulders sway as stride by stride he climbed beneath deep-fissured walls, angling among the stones and drifted domes of snow. In places he had to burrow. Armfuls of damp, slick wetness clung and melted on my neck. The man went on. The house was not half so near as he had said. There was a time I thought I had a glimpse of it; a vague light blinked and faded. Through a cleft within the rock I saw a star.

At last I drowsed. Neither sleeping nor awake, I felt the floating vastness of the night but, jostled over the high places of the earth, whether the night was above or under me I could not tell. Little pleased to lurch among the crags, the wind blew fitfully. I felt the cold and pulled myself awake. Near me everything seemed clear, but in the distance the blackness wavered like shapes in dreams. It was hard to look. Wearied, perhaps I slept again though it may be I had forgotten to close my eye. Though I had not sought him, Ar Elon's face slipped into my mind. Thrown on its side, the bloodstained head was halved and bubbling. In a pool of its own blood, it fell away in sticky clumps. The sea, I thought, has eaten him. And someone else. I tried to think. But who the other was I did not know.

More often I heard the sharp, thin clack of hooves; heard, though now I was full of sleep, the bleating cries of crowding phantoms that leapt and butted near his legs. He walked among them easily. He showed no fear. Softly, humming to himself, he called out names.

The trail seemed endless, the night as long. Worst of all, the bad air reeked of wool. Oily, soaking into flesh and hair, it filled my pores, took form and weight against my itching back. I yawned and, turning, threw out my arm. I felt it sink within a mound that spread and sagged like the prickly softness of a myrtle bog. Startled, I opened my eye. From a dozen windows the light of morning, glimmering yellow on the sills, poured down on me and lit the golden fuzz of piles of wool where for uncounted hours I had sprawled asleep.

I was in the house, though because of its unbroken height from floor to ceiling, it seemed more like a barn. From a fire pit in the center a blue coil of smoke curled upward, crossing the great blank space between until it was sucked into the morning through a deep hole in the thatch. A quarter of the floor was cut away, sunk into a stone-paved stell below, wide itself as a paddock and reached by a ramp, where huge sheep milled sedately or worried in the wooden cribs for hay. The remainder of the floor was divided roughly into thirds, the largest given over to a sort of kitchen, strewn with old iron cauldrons, ladles, mugs and knives. In the center was a thick worm-eaten table. Laddered between the windows were racks of shelves lined with brown large bowls, a score of ram skulls and, near the bottom, a great many moldy books in cracked leather bindings. The rest was fairly evenly halved between a bedroom study where the white limewashed walls were hung with what seemed maps, though of no lands I knew, and pushed into a wide corner and behind a row of all-purpose chests, a woolroom. It was there among the rugs of fleece that I looked out. The dry wool, far from the fire, was cold. I shivered.

"You might come and warm yourself," the old man said. Dressed in a simple longshirt rolled to his elbows, he crouched near the fire, adding one log and then another and another, each with different hands. He was the equal of my height and though his strength, it seemed, was greater, it was the strength of a mortal man. Age had seared his looks and bent his back. His large face was plain, his thin smile dogged as an old hill farmer's. In one hand he had a shank of mutton which, when spitted, he laid carefully across the flames.

"I am a cotter," he said afterward.

"Whose man?" I asked.

He grinned. "None I know of."

He did not seem to understand. "To whom," I said, "do you owe wool and service?"

His mild brown eyes, large under wiry brows, seemed suddenly annoyed. He scratched his ear. "No man," he said at last and turned and then turned back. "I do hope you like mutton," he began but just as quickly paused. "Though," he said, "as that is all there is, no doubt you will have it anyway."

I stood up so he could look at me, thinking my dark looks might drive some sense into him.

"I am Finn," I said, "Ar Elon's heir."

But he only gave me a worried stare and shook his head.

"No, lord," he called out firmly. "He is the one man clearly you are not."

5.

There was no sweet smell of roasting meat. After many minutes in the fire the flesh was neither singed nor blistered. The shy smoke shrank from it. The cotter pulled himself up slowly and, unconcerned, he ambled off, returning some time later with a greater load of split dry wood. When he had replenished the fire, he sat cross-legged before the pit. Puffing up his cheeks, he blew into the ash. Soon a new fire peeped out of the coals and found its voice. Like a red bird it flapped and sang. With gathered strength, great wings of flame rose up again and beat the air. Sweating against the heat, the man slid back. And yet not one drop of grease fell on the wood. The cotter gazed at the cold mass of uncooked meat. Showing no particular interest, he chewed his thumb.

I watched him carefully. Yet nothing happened. So I rose and seeing no other course but to share his company, I made a place beside him on the floor. My clothes were stiff. Hardened overnight, they smelled of salt and rubbed my wounds. Though I tried to give no sign of it, he heard me sigh.

"It is no little thing," he said, "to reach this island."

"What choice has a drowning man?" I said. "My ship foundered. The land was near."

He grinned. "No choice at all. He drowns."

"I lived."

He nodded slightly. "Your death, my lord, was always fire."

"And the sword," I said bitterly, "and drowning after." He did not answer. I set my chin in my palm. I stroked the place where my rough hair had always been. He saw the sudden strangeness in my eyes. Shifting, he laid two great hands on me. They fumbled, meaning comfort, on my back. With tar and broom he had salved the sores of all his flocks. It may be he knew no poultice for a man. Quietly, as though he had no wish for the sheep to hear, he said, "It was a bearded man I stopped, that I left tangling in his hair and rolling backward in the surf."

I stared.

"In truth," he said, "he was one like that." He cleared his throat. "And a corpse already, though we fought." He looked at me. "Still," he said, "I never let the groaning dead come on the shore. In the night with the wild wind rising from the south and west they crawl up on the stones and scare poor sheep. Then it is a wonder I get them back to feed."

Somewhere beneath the floor an old ram stamped his hooves. "Aye," the cotter went on softly and clutched my hands, "that one was bearded, his black hair twisted with the white, all snarled with salt, a corpse already. Not a sheared, fair lad the like of you."

He stopped and in the silence I could hear the useless breathing of the fire, the mutton cold. I looked down and saw my own pale flesh, white as any of the children of Kell, saw it out of two clear eyes, as I had not seen anything since I climbed the windy stair about Gwen Gildrun, before the crow. Now with both eyes I drank in the brightness of the morning, the licking fire, the crouched six-handed man, his old neck twisted round to look at me. He saw my fear.

"Twice," he said quietly, "the men you are no longer tried to reach the shore. They could not come to it. This was no place for them. Here no living man may walk, nor, until all is ready, can the dead."

In the sheath of flesh that was not mine I shivered. "You live," I said, "here where by your words . . ." Reeling, I stopped and shut my eyes. Yet beneath the lids I saw him. He drew a breath. The fire so newly lit had dwindled to a single flame. Gazing into it, he raised his hand, but touching nothing, let it fall.

"For ages I have sat upon the rocks," he said, "and watched the corpses floating in. So long in the sea, they have no strength to harm a man but they kill with grief. So Finn pitied the corpse and failed. As for Ar Elon, he had only forgotten he was dead. Myself, I did no more than hold him back till he remembered."

"Then what am I?" I whispered helplessly.

"The son."

"Whose?"

"Ar Elon's," he said and scratched his ear. "Finn's."

"Surely . . ."

He shook his head. His long sad face was pained. "I swore to serve you, lord," he said. "But there are mornings in the world I rue it." Within him something snapped. He stood up suddenly. "By your leave, I'll fetch the third damn load of wood," he said, "burn the mutton one last time and have my breakfast."

After he had eaten he was gone, calling the sheep out of the stell and driving them through the broad doors into the air. I knew nothing of sheep. Yet it did not seem the dumb beasts, impatient and nudging each other's sides, had sensed his anger. He chanted over them, singing a strange discordant insolent melody. The ill sound scraped their backs, scattering and rebounding like pebbles thrown against a wall. Then as suddenly he fell silent. But the sheep kept on with the noise he started, the tuneless chant returning to him, tranquil and with a fullness he had not given it as though nothing pleased sheep more than wandering out to pasture on cold rock and crusted snow. The last ewe tossed her halfwit's head. With a haughty look she passed the threshold.

When the house was still, I tried the meat. The third time in the fire indeed had roasted it; but the flesh was stringy and I put it aside before I had my fill. I remembered the carcasses the old men of the towns beneath our holding, too lame to hunt, had sometimes brought in for the pot. Though stewed all day, such meat had never truly softened. He did not butcher this, I thought; he found it dead. Yet, bewildered, I remembered he had said no dead could come upon this land.

He is a fool, I thought. At the same time I tried not to think, for the talk of other selves had frightened me. Yet, though I would not, I remembered the quiet corpse that I had buried in the sea, remembered though it was not my memory, the other, his full lips black as a mare's, his long hair wet upon his back. Though I did not want to look, I saw him mount the beach again on splayed webbed feet, saw, as a man sees himself, out of his own eyes, the six-armed giant standing up ahead. I waved the thing away and clenched my teeth.

At that moment I saw the basin.

It was round and deep, the match of the one the Mughain's women had set out for me. It had been left on the table, the knives and crockery placed aside. Warily, I lifted it. A faint sweat broke out on my brow.

Out of my cloak I took the flask. I did not hurry. There were no eyes on me to make me awkward. When I had settled the basin in my lap, I hunched my shoulders over it. Then slowly, I poured the clear Hren

water into its depths. The surface shimmered. The
white light from the windows reflected in my face. I
waited, expecting the beaded light to dance, the bands
of brightness to twist and snake, to burst like small
choked veins, a swollen world of mist and smoke beneath. So on Tywy it happened. I did not move. Yet it
was only the same quiet room I saw and at its center a
man, his pale hands tightening on the edges of a metal
bowl. His white hair hung at his shoulders. Out of deep
gray startled eyes I watched him blink.

I stood outside the door looking over the hard,
dormant fields that edged the house. Against the snow
the sky was brilliant. But in the yard the drifts were
trampled, muddied and turned to slop by hooves. The
rutted track ran west below the walls, turned through
an ancient gate and disappeared. I wondered if there
was any good in running after him. Though at first he
had seemed gentle, even cheerful, it had not seemed
much like friendship at the end. Yet he had sworn, he
had said, to serve me. But sworn to whom? He had not
sworn, I knew, to me.

I moved off the step and into the yard, not yet
following him, only moving. Beyond the gate the path
plunged toward the sea. An immense wall ran along the
hill, its great height sloping back until I was not certain
that I saw its summit. Its shaping must have been
outside memory, for everywhere I looked the old foun-
dations were breached and crumbled. Here and there
boulders the size of oxen had fallen out of place and
filled the path. The wall itself had been dug away
behind them. But even in these delvings I never saw
bare earth but only layered stones of inner walls as
though not only the spurs and ridges of the hills were
stonework but the whole prodigious island one great
fortress made with hands. Despite my cares, I smiled to

think of it, imagining so vast a holding that mountains were its towers or that the barren fields that checkered out of sight across the hills were no more in fact than tiles laid thick along its roof. I wondered where I got such thoughts. It did not matter they were foolishness. They warmed my heart, settled for a moment the wild strange shapes into things I knew.

The path twisted. I wedged myself around the stones, marveling how the old man had carried me through such narrowness, how in the morning he drove his flocks back through them. Loose stones scuffled at my feet, rolled over the edge, and hurtled soundlessly into the pit below. It was the space of several breaths before I heard the thin, far sound when finally they struck the ice. Thereafter I kept more closely to the wall.

I walked until the sun was high above the island, until the shadows that had shriveled began to grow again. The path dropped dangerously. Still, I was high up when the wall fell back, leaving open country straight ahead. Down a mile, to either side of a short bent crag, I saw the shingled beach where I had come ashore. The tide was out. White specks of sheep were straggling across the stones, their small heads browsing in the pools for weed. The sea was well beyond them, stretching gray and definite toward a far clear edge. If there were other isles and kingdoms in the West, even from this place, with two good eyes, I could not see them. I plodded on.

The river that all day I had followed at a distance now was near. Because I thirsted, I left the track. I slithered down the slope, fumbling over sliding stones, and came at last with several bruises to the bank. Out of a drift I worked a stone. When I had freed it, I cast it at the ice. After several tries the hard ice splintered but the water was so cold it stung. Then for several minutes, catching my breath, I waited.

The day had been still, with no air moving. Now as evening came, a cold mist drifted inland from the sea. Though I was weary, I found I had to hurry on to keep from freezing. I went along the bank, my hands shoved deep inside my shirt for warmth. I dug my fingers against the skin and felt the strange hair prickling, the thick nubs of nipples. I went on, but an odd uneasiness went with me. Whosesoever flesh this was, it was not my own.

I thought, I am the son. The word was meaningless.

When I had come out onto the beach, the flocks were moving in. The tide had turned and followed them. The surf was building. I heard the dim air boom against the cliffs. I stared. Yet, however long I looked, it still seemed monstrous, each wave like a wall of headless men, their torsos fused, flinging their bound flesh in endless rage against the stone. The great rocks tore them to shreds. At their backs the sun was setting. The sea was red.

In some other life, now done with, or some life yet to come, I heard or would hear old women lisping tales across the looms. Their dry tongues move like shuttles clicking back and forth, telling the daughters of the house how it was on such nights in winter, the old sun dying, the new moon hooked and dangling in the heaven's ear, that the young brown sealmen rose out of the freezing bay and taking manshapes danced and warmed themselves upon the shore. Their manes and shoulders would, they said, have glittered like the foam. Hidden in the rocks, the lonely landwives, watching, ached with joy.

Alone, I waited, restless and staring at the wastes of stone, feeling the evening creep in. A grim moon edged above the hills but brought no light. In the lowering dark the cold sheep stirred and bleated. Once more, uncertain, I ran my eyes along the beach, across its desolate faults and muddy terraces, but no youths danced. The sea was blank, a lake of old dead men. It flung up corpses. I found no joy in it and muttered to myself. Better should I have been had I stayed in Tywy, I thought. There at least I might have fought the death they offered me.

The cotter was nowhere to be seen. Indeed, with darkness falling, it grew ever harder to see anything at all. One gets used to light, to the coming and going of servants with brands and candles. At Morrigan my mother always set some women by the fire to rake and poke it. In that house there were always whispers; even down the darkest corridor, a cough, the sound of footsteps hurrying.

He will not be far away, I thought, nor gone beyond the hearing of his flocks. So I went to stand where the sheep were huddled in the damp. They watched me, each black head lifted, the round eyes searching and afraid. The cold night deepened. The surf crashed endlessly.

Then all at once the crests of waves were wrinkling with the radiance of stars. The beach turned silver and the moon seemed bright. From the cliff behind me the sound of laughter boomed. I whirled around.

A gate rose shining up against the rock. Between the posts the shadow of a cave sank back from sight. Laughing, holding his sides with one great pair of hands, the cotter strode out briskly from the hill. Despite the cold, his face was sleek with sweat. He had a long-handled mallet in his arms and in his hands a spike and several shovels. A length of straw rope was trailing loose about his neck. Relieved, my heart leapt when I looked at him. Yet I had my pride.

"Why do you laugh?" I said.

He turned, bewildered for a moment, to see me there. The mirth went out of him. "You have no cause

to spy on me," he said. "When the work is done, I'll
see you hear of it." His voice was harsh, yet I had not
expected the resentment in his eyes.

"I did not come to spy," I said.

"You came."

"The house was empty. I gave no thought to what
you did."

His old head tilted, stiffened, the anger suddenly
going from his stare. Yet for the look he gave me I
might have struck him with a whip. I did not understand the change in him. "Perhaps I am too old," he
said, "too old and too feeble for your will." His grim
mouth closed, then opened awkwardly. "Yet I have
done the best I could. The work is dreary. Long, you
know, I've been at it." He stopped but went on staring.
"And what harm is there if, when I am free of it, I
laugh?" His face was set. Still, it was the face of a man
who grieves.

I shook my head. "I was alone."

He frowned.

"So you have always been," he answered gloomily.
"And so you shall be until I've done."

He turned and called out roughly to his flocks.
Though I tried to think of words to say to him, I did not
find them.

I could not climb the hills again. I stood still, unwill-
ing but of anger to say as much, but knowing that if on
the way I stumbled I would never let him take me on
his back. The cotter shambled up and down, his old
sides heaving. Wistfully he looked off at the distant
peaks. Yet he did not go. Finally, whistling sharply
through his teeth, he drove the sheep against the cliff,
turned them—whistling louder—until they pressed into
the wide mouth of the cave. They went in gladly,
untroubled by the dark. Muttering, he stood by the

post until the last had passed him. "Come on, then," he said to me. Still I lagged and by the time I followed, having fumbled with something in his cloak, he had a taper lit. With that small light he set fire to several torches he had gathered up with a spare hand and, moving methodically about the room, had put them into brackets on the wall.

I stopped at the entrance, a great bare hall opening in front of me, and gawked. It was no sea-cave but manwork, delved and cut back deeply in the hill. Thick columns, naked, without paint or carving, rose at either side to support the ceiling. The span between was empty. At the back a broad archway led away again into the dark. I stood and looked. The old man, knowing the place, stared back at me. He drew no nearer.

"This portal will be last," he said. "It is not finished." There was a tone in the cotter's voice that might have been annoyance, or might have been the mask of it.

"Within," he said, "are nine times ninety halls."

"And at its heart?"

His brown eyes flashed. "A maze of tunnels, lord," he said, "long twisting passages, vaults and rooms."

"And under them?"

"The dark."

I saw, I imagined nothing. Yet, far from its beginning or its end, I found a thread. "But in the deepest place?" I asked.

He smiled. "A throne."

Like rain upon parched land a joy washed over me. It had no cause, no reason. No form or color crossed my mind, no glimmering of stones, no fine gold glittering. A coolness only touched my memory. And yet I felt a vastness risen underneath the hill: cold, invisible, too huge for any man, and yet a throne. Not knowing why, I laughed.

There was a man beside me in the hall. He laid the

mallet and the spike aside, left them leaning with his shovels on the wall.

"Then you are pleased?" he said.

I looked about once more, uncertain, remembering there was light, and saw that there before me were two plain chairs, cut from the rock, not shadows, and a fire pit with wood already stacked and waiting on the floor. A small square table had been dragged before it. On its back were two deep cups and at the edge a jar. "You knew that I would come," I said.

"Surely there would be one of you."

I felt the blood rise in my neck. "Which one am I?"

"Llugh," he answered softly, "the shining one, the white."

I shook my head.

He heard my halting breath and sighed. "How should you remember? When the shapes that once had held you walked the land, Géar had not her son." He scratched his ear. "Truly, lord, what child has heard his name before his birth?" He turned and, going to the fire pit, lit the wood. The flames danced up between the stones. I watched him silently.

When he had heated the wine, he brought a cup and put it roughly in my hands. I did not feel it. For a heartbeat in the shadow of an oak I had seen her dark eyes laughing. I knew it was another place. It was only a moment, but I spilled the wine. One red drop slid gently between my fingers. "Is it for Llugh," I said, "you cut into the hill?"

He reached out for the cup. "No." The word was bitter. Hard as a stone it flew against the wall.

"You serve me."

"I serve the three who came."

"Two are dead."

He shrugged. "I am too stupid to argue with you, lord. Who am I to know your ways? Build the hall, you say. I built it." His sad old peasant's face had darkened. He looked away.

The silence, that had lain always at our backs, crept forth and sat between us.

Later, propped against a chair, he slept. Outside the slow pulse of the breakers filled the night. For a moment I stood over him, considering the old head, the square mass of his shoulders. His hands were open. Stretched across his belly, the long scarred fingers twitched. Even dreaming, without hope, now without thought, he kept at his work.

I stepped across the fire. The flames stirred briefly with my passing, then settled back. They gave no light to the room beyond. Out of the bracket on the wall I took a torch.

6.

The cotter sat before his table, his arms sprawled over the parchment, working with three hands. He held his head cocked to one side, intent, unhearing. The quills moved back and forth from the inkwells. He did not turn until I had closed the door, until I had mounted the well-worn steps and stood unsteady at his back.

"Are you satisfied?" he asked quietly.

I unclasped my wet cloak and let it sink beside me to the floor. A smear of dampness spread along the stones, grew into puddles. He did not notice. Over his shoulders I could see the small black marks he had been making on the parchment. They were clustered all in one corner, near the edge, like a dozen irregular chips of glass. He did not wait to hear my answer but turned again to stare at them himself. He had been drawing islands.

"I was lost," I said.

A hard rain whitened the windows. When I had climbed the hill from the shore it had been snow, a thick suffocating snow blown in gusts and mixed with thunder. Against the winter sky the outline of mountains had melted into a fog, a cold miasmic damp that clung to my eyes and webbed my lungs. Before me and behind the drifted path had tumbled off in mist. I was in the air again. But I had not been less afraid. It had been no different underground, my hands fumbling on the rock, feeling the darkness slip away invisibly.

"The first room," I said unevenly, "branched into three others, those three each to three again. And so it went on endlessly." He sat staring at his parchment. "The torch," I said, "burned out."

He moved his eyes back to my face. "And the throne?"

But then I could not bear to look at him. I held on fiercely to his chair, feeling the thin chill roots of fear drive through my blood. The corner of my lip caught on my teeth. "I was lost," I said. "I told you. There was only darkness."

He got up slowly, easing himself away from the table. "Come to the fire," he said, his old hands moving firmly under my arms to steady me. His face was drawn.

"Tell me who you are," I said.

"Why?"

"Because I ask."

He frowned. "My lord, you are weary."

Stiffening, I looked back at him. "I would hear your answer."

He was silent awhile, his head lifted, like one who sees what he had thought was gone. The deep haggard line of his mouth pulled thinly at the edge. "Fir Dhearga," he said. I saw him smile. "So the first kings called me when they walked on land. But they who called me so are gone. That name went with them." His lips closed for a moment while he thought. "Thereafter I had many names, though there was none but myself to hear them. Now, if you will listen, you will hear it is Mug Dafad the bold sheep name me. In their pride, my lord, they take me for their servant." His red brows arched. I meant to press him but he sat me down beside the fire, so close the flames licked near my legs. "Aye," he said, "perhaps that name is best."

The stench of burning blew into my face. I scowled. "If you know me, you know I find no warmth in this!"

He laughed outright. "Lord," he said, "though I have tried to think, it is hard to know what you remember."

I did not like the sound but the fire was hot. It took my breath. Sweating, with what strength I had I fumbled with my shirt. I had tugged it half off my back when a tear in the damp cloth tangled in my hair and caught. Silently, needing his help, I said his name. He sat unmoving.

"You"—I said aloud—"you I have forgotten utterly."

"I know," he said. "Yet I have not." The words came whispered through his teeth. I felt his hand.

Freed from the shirt, I stared up at him.

A dark wind buffeted the house, hurling rain like spearheads against the windows. So the winter storms had beat against the ledges, drumming on the panes at Morrigan. I strove not to think of it and yet I remembered how at Morrigan it was more often snow. There even in full summer the wind blew cold, coming from the west, from the landless reaches of the sea. I remembered standing on the landing outside Urien's door, before the mullioned windows and looking over the ridge, out over the sloping shoulders of our mountain. Sweeping across the summit, the storms had draped the fields with tatters of linen, with long and prickly cloaks of deep, white wool. I had not moved. A voice was murmuring. Through the locked door of his chamber Urien cried out as he read from the books of the wars. I heard it clearly.

Mug Dafad turned his head.

The voice melted; the fire sprang up again, blistering my face.

"Llugh?" he asked but I was done with madness.

"I am myself!" I panted. "From Géar Finn, from the rough peaks of the mountain I have my name." The flames shone glittering through the white mane of my hair. I pushed the strands aside and swore.

Mug Dafad leaned back on two long arms. "And?"

"Nor shall I lose it."

He looked out past me, across the emptiness of his house, out through the streaming windows toward the sea. The storm had not given up its hammering.

"It is too soon," he said above the noise. "Though why, being unready, you chose to come I do not understand." He shrugged. "Yet who," he said, "has ever known just what you wanted?" He stood for a moment wordlessly. It seemed to me he grieved.

"Come, lord," he said at last. "I have saved your sword. The night you came I fished it from the deep. Nor have I let your great ship come to ruin. Even now it lies waiting outside the reef."

Unbelieving I stared at him. "The storm still rages."

"Lord," he interrupted me, "who would stop you if you meant to stay?" He smiled. "Tomorrow, surely, will be soon enough. But while the storm lasts I must teach you how to cross the sea again. It is long since you came out of the west and the way is hard." He paused. "The more so," he added, "since you will not remember what you know."

He left the fire. "Come," he said, "all this night I have been working on charts and drawing islands."

They have dragged the chair out into the air where I can watch the beach. The armorers hover at my right hand, fondling my weapons like children with new toys. They are afraid, and yet I see their eagerness. Long they have heard of my victories, how I humiliated the barons at Dineiden, how like a bull in battle I have warded the land. Still, it is only weird airs and old man's talk to them. They are too young to have seen it.

The place where we have gathered rustles with new-budded leaves. Slowly the wood has crept back, the shattered limbs cleared and saplings grown tall in their place. I remember the women, their naked breasts red in the last light of evening; many are now in their graves.

The shadow of the leaves speckles the arms of the boys. There are patches in the growth where I can see ahead. It will be a long day, I think. All around me I hear the clink of weapons, the men swearing softly because of the flies.

Njal, my youngest, lifts my sword. It is the first time he has carried it. His fingers linger on the hilt. "Who now can doubt your strength?" he says proudly. "Never have I heard that so many came at a king's summoning. There is not a hall that doesn't stand empty, not a field where the men haven't left off their plowing."

Grown trees stand over us. I look down at my hands. "I was alone when first I came here," I answer quietly. "Then this place was a deep old wood." I smile. "I had none to help me then and yet alone I made a field of it. Mag Finn, they named it."

There is no need to say more to him. He is Unn's child; his hair has the same gold color hers had once. Alike he has her cunning. He sees this aged scarred face, these heavy bones jutting under yellowed flesh.

"The years have not been unkind," he murmurs softly. "Each season has brought increase of glory. Never, I swear it, have I seen such a force." He is looking out over the crouching backs of the soldiers. "Now you have only to raise your hand."

The young men near us draw themselves up trying to make their ghost-white faces look less frightened, to seem as brave as Njal's words would have them. With

new oaths they have promised to protect at any cost the
body of their king.

"It is an army of boys I have," I tell him. "Better I
would have liked it if I had Ceorl with me."

He is looking over the water. "Who am I to remind
you, lord?" he says. "Yet all men die. Only the king
goes on and on."

"Still, I would have wished him here."

Something in his face pleads quiet, but he laughs. "It
is only a boy," he says, "who comes over the waves to
fight with you."

He has not yet given me the sword. I lay my hand
beside his on the hilt. I say, "He is my son."

Njal's tanned, large face is streaked with dust. He
does not move. Along the western horizon the faint
bland shadow of a cloud seems hardly to advance. Its
distant lightning forks noiselessly. Somehow the cloud is
nearer.

"He is my heir," I say, "the first child of my loins."

His fingers stick against the hilt. His breath is harsh.

But already the sentinels have seen the first bright
sails. "Llugh comes!" they cry out in warning and
alarm. On the strand and back into the trees the
landsmen take up the cry. The wood is filled with
unsurpassed, unbelievable roaring.

"You must strive to look more kingly," Mug Dafad
said.

He had given me a new longshirt embroidered with
vines, bright green leaves and berries. Though snug
across the shoulders, it fitted well enough, I thought.
The useless armholes could always be resewn. The
white long cloak was trimmed with ermine and clasped
with bronze. Three buckles of silver he had fastened to
my waist. Into one hand he put a gaudy shield and
under my left arm the rolled parchment, bound in a

sheath of kid and secured with seven gold coils of chain. Almost I felt like the barons who stood at Thigg's call at Ormkill. Surely a man could not fight so dressed. I wriggled.

Mug Dafad's deep eyes looked hard at mine. "The Penandrun are old," he said. "Pray their sight is not so keen as once it was." He took his old hand from my back and winked. "Fear nothing. A stiff wind will blow away the smell of sheep."

Wavelets clucked against the hull, the rigging creaked. He took, I saw, some joy in that. He said, "You have only to go as I taught you, westward where the sea and sky make one gray line. Yet if all else fails, as each day closes, sail at the sun."

I strain to tell it—even now, though six score times I've said the words and, after a dozen tellings, more or less the same. Though not in the hall. Not among such men as earn their drink with tales, men who have whole histories in their heads, though they speak cold-heartedly, who know not only what last Urien said to me but where he spoke and what it meant and the name, god knows, of the first star shining that night when evening came. To them I dare not tell anything, not that didn't happen one, two, three toward death or with a leap into the bed of a woman. I told a red-haired farmer down in Harl, told it twice, in fact, because I bought the wine. He thought there should be more about the sheep. Say what you will.

In a crofter's hut, the houseman twisting twigs of heather, his fat wife spinning, I told it backward. In truth, it made no sense to him. Still we laughed and the houseman, seeing the poverty of his table, pushed his daughter at me in place of ale. Afterward, while she pinched fleas against her thighs, I told it straight. She did her best to seem polite but knew, she said, a livelier tale about a wheelwright who met a female bogey on the road to Tyre.

Say what you will. The world is wide and if death is wider, yet eternity has but a narrow door.

White the island was and barren. So even in the books of the wars it is written. It rose from the gray ocean like a floating town, half-made, like a citadel whose roofs were mountain rock, whose deepest heart was darkness. Old it was as the rocking sea and hollowed like a hall. Three times I tried to climb upon the shore. Twice, staggering against the surf, against shapes I might have dreamt, I fell back witless. The third time an immense old man found the thing I was, alone and shaking on the stones. Like senseless mutton he strapped me in his house. Some days I spent there. No man was witness to what we said. But when I left, my hair was white and I had both my eyes. Under my arm I bore a rolled-up map of islands in the West.

The old men cough. The young men smile behind their hands.

"You mites! You flies!" I scream at them. "When you come knocking, if I will not have you, who is there to let you in?"

7.

It is no great matter getting used to other flesh. Ever boys shoot up, thickening what once was lean. So youths turn men and old men, sleeping by the wall, grow fat. Yet no arm remembers that its reach was less. The flesh scarce knows the thoughts of men. With me it was no different. In three days I had forgotten I had all my sight and saw, without regarding it, like other men. The gray clouds drifted west across the bow. I lived; the blood worked in my veins. Though they were not my legs, such as they were, they held me when I stood. It was only in the evenings I remembered Llugh.

In dreams, on the island that rose only in sleep, Géar held him out to me, her white arms lifted above the waves. I saw the child, wrapped in a dirty rag and crying for the sea. He inspired no terror. In truth such dreaming convinced me I had little yet to fear from him. Only Géar bewildered me. I saw her walking on the shore, her white face radiant as she watched the boy. For that I grieved. Bitterly, I considered the faithlessness of women, who will be made happy by a squalling babe in dirty linen.

But in the days I had no time to think of her. I was alone. It needed twenty men, I thought, to keep the sails.

The first rigging Mug Dafad set, and while that served well enough when the wind was at my back, out of the smell of land, the breeze turned around. The ocean heaved up sliding hills, the sleek sails tore and there was nothing I could do but drop the lines. Those I could not free, for the deck pitched under me, I cut through with my sword. But even then the broad ship rolled. To keep from falling I crawled back to sit on the bench beneath the awning. A far-off grayness wrapped the sun. I folded my arms and watched the rolling ocean cover it.

A child of the land imagines there is an infinite horizon out at sea, a vastness proclaiming immortality. Yet how small the world seems from the deck. With no height greater than the mast to climb, the bravest sailor looks at best a few short leagues ahead. Far better then is a house on a blowing hill. When night and storm come prowling, a man can always bar the door.

The ship rocked fretfully. In time I slept. When I awoke the wind was running through my flesh. Unrested still, I leaned against the rail. The tail of some dream lashing in my head, I was not listening. Yet the air, it seemed, was filled with belling cries. I turned my head.

From the north and east the water all about was black with seals. Barking with grief, they crowded near the ship. Thrusting up their chiseled heads, they gasped for air. Their bleak eyes found me on the deck, stared with such mad fright when they saw me that I looked away, looked past them to where the sea was blank.

Yet there was something.

Black, two fathoms deep, a wrinkling shadow moved beneath the waves. It had no form, no more than night has, yet it advanced unceasingly as night advances. With awful certainty the shadow passed beneath their outer ranks.

The mobbed seals wailed. I caught their fear—not of

the dark itself but of the stillness out ahead of it, the uneasy quiet before the blackness slithered up to sight. I tugged my cloak. Straining with my neck, I felt the vast head rising with my own.

Hill-like, mossed and scaled, horribly it cut the air. The head split wide. I saw the rows of dagger teeth. Already reddened, a seal corpse lay mangled in its mouth. There was a grim, brief silence. Chunks of lifeless meat bobbed in the sea.

The huge tail slapped. With bleeding jaws it lumbered in once more. Ten thousand flippers scratched; ten thousand scrambled. Black, splattered bodies rolled down headless in the waves. I heard its roar. As though in answer, a cry out of my own chest coursed through the ship. The long boards shuddered, pulled against their ribs, and squealed. Clamping shut my eyes, I jerked away. But, even blind, I felt my clawed great fingers rake on flesh. Against my teeth a throbbing belly came apart.

I forced my eyelids open.

The sea had fallen. I did not understand, nor did I want to understand it, now. I shook my head.

Beyond the bow, sculling with his webbed black hands, a seal was watching me. His coat was bright beneath the stars, without a wound. About him were the corpses of his kin. "Lord," he called up solemnly, "why do you let us die?"

Unknowing what I had done or not done, my voice was cold. "How have I wronged you?" I called to him. "Myself, I never sought your life."

His clear eyes, black as currants, shone with grief. "What does it matter what you sought? Over the sea we saw a great ship shining and we came. But what seemed light welled into darkness and night devoured us."

I looked away. "Surely, there is safety somewhere. The sea is wide."

"Not wide enough."

I clutched the rail. I said, "What is it that you want?"

He grunted bitterly. "Only tell us, lord, where you are not."

There was a dryness at my heart. I strove to touch it. But out of my own flesh, even as I roared, the Darkness that had been only waiting came.

"White he is—like some ice hill," the voice said stubbornly.

The other swore. "As are some seals," he said.

The faces I could barely see looked down at me.

"Yet he is a man."

"So we were once."

"And yet, lord, he is a man and white."

The other spat. "Then you must ask him what he is."

The smaller paused. His long nose whiskers twitched. "He sleeps," he said.

But I sat up, to look at them. The greater snorted. Begrudgingly he moved a ponderous flipper just out of reach. Thereafter he did not stir. His head was large, not quite a seal's nor yet a man's. In the dampness, though the wind had roughened it, his coat was silver; his dark eyes shone, brighter than mortal eyes. I set my teeth.

"Where is the Dark?" I said.

The smaller swallowed twice before he spoke. "Man," he answered, "already it is night."

I looked across the rail. The sea and sky were all one dimness, with no clear line between. But if it were night, it was a night without stars. The ship moved softly through a mist.

"There were seals," I said.

The smaller stared uneasily. "There are always seals."

"No," I said, "the sea was black with them."

The other, who had not spoken at all to me, was

quiet, his remote eyes turned back to watch the waves. "Twelve days we swam alone," he said, his deep voice low, "and there was nothing before us or behind and nothing on either side."

I looked at him and past him. Indeed the sea was empty, the corpses gone. "Then it was only a dream," I said, relieved. "I am glad of that. Had it been otherwise I would have owed you whatever blood-price is due your rank."

His bull neck straightened. "Then, man, you would have owed me much. In my own country I was king."

He shambled nearer, his blunt nails scraping on the deck. His great bulk overhung me like a ledge. Yet, looking up, I smiled. "That is an odd thing surely," I answered him, "for I was king myself of the only land I know." So that I would have my height again, I stood. He took no notice.

"What land?" he said.

"Tir rhwng Moroedd, the land between the seas."

"Just one more island." His proud lip curled. "What claim is that to grandness? There is no lack of islands."

I smiled again. "It is not from the land my kingship comes."

The sealman scowled. "Say then who you are," he said.

He saw me pause.

"By Dagda," he said dryly, "either you are someone or you are not."

I waited, though there was no cause for it. Since I had gone into the world, so men had challenged me. And freely I had answered, taking good care that all should hear, a name that I had shouted before the Menhir, before swordsmen and tinkers, before Thigg himself and all his hosts and heralds in my father's hall. Even to Mug Dafad, though he had muttered, I had sworn it. Yet now I stood looking down at my white hands. The mist blew cold and damp across my nostrils. It had the smell of darkness on it, the urine smell of fear. I bent my head. The air rushed by me. It smelled, I knew, of the blood of seals.

"I am Finn," I told him.

The sealman nodded.

"I am Llugh, the son of Finn."

His dark stare hardened; his face became a stone.

"I am Ar Elon," I whispered, "though he is dead." My voice trailed off.

I stopped, for already I had said more than I knew. Yet the words, having found shape in my mouth, seemed hard as fact. Three deaths I would have, Cerridwen said. Three lives, then, were mine as well. Yet there was something more. Fragments, pieces making nothing whole, jerked in my head. It was as when from the door at Cerridwen's hut I had looked north and south at once, on darkness and morning, as the old stone turned, except surely it was the stone that was still, the great earth wheeling around instead. I could not find my place. My head was spinning.

The sealman grunted. I lifted my neck.

As far as his bulk would let him I saw him kneel. The smaller followed, his webbed short fingers spread in homage, his weak unseeing eyes bent toward the deck. But the eyes of the other were hard and still. He watched me carefully.

"It is little enough joy I have had since I took this shape," he said. "No more will this bring me. There is no help for it. The world goes as it must." He straightened awkwardly. "Lord," he whispered, his low voice certain as it was dismayed, "you have my service and, as far as I may give it, that of my servant."

I thought of all the men who once had sworn to me, to me as to Ar Elon they had sworn.

"What name did you know?" I said.

He frowned: a king himself though bound in a beast's
rank flesh, half one thing and half another, even as I
was, shared among my lives.

"The one name," he answered evenly, "you would
not say."

The men are gone, frightened like dogs of thunder,
slinking from the hall, not looking back. Even he who
must attend the king has gotten himself safe beyond the
doors. In the grim light of the little fires I give them I
see he has gone off without his pike. He hasn't, I know,
the stomach to come back for it. I think, How will there
be courage in the land when the heart of the king is
mad? It is a good thought worth repeating, worth
telling the *filidh* when, their bellies empty, they creep
back with the light . . . like hounds, I think, whose only
bravery is their bellies' growl. Poor hounds, I think,
frightened by an old king telling tales.

"Do you fear me as well?" I ask her.

Half-listening, she brushes her old woman's hair off
her face. "What are your lies to me?" she answers
quietly. "I who bore your children?" Her voice is tired,
the shrillness muted by a yawn. It is an old argument,
more habit now than anger. "Was there a night," she
sighs, "I didn't hear your whisperings?"

Her thin arms folded, she passes among the deserted
benches. "Your ravings," she runs on softly, "and shouting
to old dead men." She stoops, resting her cheek against
the cool stones of the hearth. "The guests gone from my
house—men who came out of kindness, out of faith to
honor us." She touches, wearily, the hilt of my sword
where it hangs from its brace by the logs and kettles.
She turns her head.

"My lord, are you certain it is Llugh who comes
against us?"

"Yes."

She rises stiffly, her flat eyes moving among the benches, seeing each place where the men are not. "How do you know?" she asks me.

"Woman, I have always known."

Her hands are clenched against her flesh. "You?" she says, her small voice dry, a whisper in the cold. But for the sentries the yards below are empty. I hear them shifting on frozen boots, watching the distance, uneasy in the chill black air. Inside, the fires at last are dead, the darkness greater than the night without. Only her eyes are bright.

"You—who were never certain?—who were always asking but never, though you walked with marvels, never asked them outright what they meant?"

"Yes."

"You knew?"

"Yes."

"What Mug Dafad built beneath the hill?" She pauses. "The name . . . ," she begins.

I lean forward, looking across the floor stones from the chair that was always mine, from which in the years before her birth I ruled this folk. There are voices in the hall, but only I can hear them. In the darkness I can almost distinguish the figures of the barons, bold men in their finery, the lean hounds sucking bones at their feet. Like brown leaves are the faces of the men who are gone. There is a stiffness in my neck. I turn. Against my shoulders the seahair bristles.

In the morning it rained. Listening, I blinked awake beneath the awning. Silver curtains shunted off from the canvas but within it was almost dry. During the night the wind had come around to the south, casting a storm before it. Still, it was unlike any rain I knew. The air was filled with a vague, weightless light. The soft rain fell without touching it, as though in one place worlds of air and water passed without meeting. I drew a breath.

At my left hand was a fish, green-scaled and silver-bellied. A trickle of blood was clotted at its mouth. The hand that had placed it there pulled away.

"I have left that," he said in a boy's cracked voice. Naked and shivering, he sat outside the awning, the rain matting his dark hair. He was small and so scrawny I might have added up his ribs. About his bare knees was a mound of heads and fishbones.

"It is poor fare," I said, staring, "that leaves you thin."

His teeth were rattling but he grinned. "Lord," he said, "I was a seal when I ate them. What good they did me that shape has." He poked his own frail arms. "Truly," he said, "I was better off with fur but the spell is hard. I keep forgetting."

I saw how pitifully he hugged himself. Drawing off my cloak, I threw it out to him. He snatched it gratefully and tugging the embroidered cloth about his shoudlers he cried out gaily. "Lord," he shouted, "I swear if ever men or seals come at you, it is Wyck you shall have at your hand."

I felt a smile half crease my mouth. "That is your name?"

He nodded.

"Then, Wyck, you have my thanks," I said and laughed for the wind was not as cold as it had been and the rain was outside the awning. With no more thought I took the fish. The meat was odd and, although I did not much like the taste of it, it made short work. "And where is your master?" I asked with my last mouthful.

Wyck's eyes which had been darting happily rested on his feet. He prodded them. "He feeds in the sea," he said, wistful all at once. "He was a mage before he was a king. There is wizardry in his marrow and salt in his veins." Still digging at his toes, he sighed. "He never forgets the words."

I had been a boy myself and heard at their spellfires the aunts, smelling at crows' rumps and muttering, quoting the old speech learned by heart, wild words I had never mastered. I frowned. Wise and sad were the women of the Kell, but one by one death took them.

"They are only words," I said.

The boy cocked his head.

The rain had darkened and a man came forth from it. Tall he was and naked as the boy. But it was the sea that ran from his shoulders. He paused at the awning, his wide nostrils sniffing the air. He looked down at the fishbones.

"I trust he left a scrap for you."

"As much as he was able."

The tall man laughed. His head was long and horselike but it had a king's steadiness. His big hands were motionless by his side. Without my leave he came under the awning.

I had not forgotten our meeting.

"What name did you swear to?" I asked. For in the night, even as he knelt, I had gone off to sleep.

Under his upper lip his horse teeth showed in a grin. "What, lord," he answered back, "accepts such an oath unknowing?"

I saw the truth of that, but thought, knowing less, brave men have sworn to me. Need comes, as unlooked for as oaths. Only a fool neglects help when it is offered. But I saw he was just. "It is as you say. It was only rudeness I gave you."

"That is a fair answer," he said. "As fair will I give you. But a tale comes with it." His eyes that were strange in a seal were stranger in a man. He did not blink as I watched them.

I said: "I will hear it."

He found a place for himself and sat, putting his big hands on his knees. "I was a king myself," he said, "of Tir na Trí Oileán, which, although they are called that, are no lands at all but only islands. The islands themselves hardly deserve to be called so. The greatest is no more than a coppice of brushwood sticking high out of the sea and the lesser but two hills off the coast. Yet I was king over them as my father was. Though, in truth, we were both kings for show. The women rule there, the king's only business hunting boars in the wood and watching the ocean."

I knew the feeling and liked him better for it. I said: "So it was when I was a boy at Morrigan."

He smiled. "Yet even that came to less. There have been many kings since the world was young, and few pigs. When I took the kingship I had only the sea to look at."

"That would be a most unkingly business," I said.

"Surely there was not much luck in it," he answered. "Still, morning and evening I walked on the shore. For as the days went, the air itself of the uplands seemed to sour in my lungs and the stone of my wife-sister's house was without glory. Far better, I thought, were the salt wind and the stones that rolled in the surf. It came even that I slept at the shore's edge. And since he was as unneeded as I, for then there was little work for his hounds, I brought my dog boy for company."

He glanced at the boy. "Even as he is now," he said, "so he was then: eager and sad by turns, small help and great trouble. Yet he would be ruled by me. So together we sat on the banks that faced westward, upon the great ocean, watching the dolphins leap and the small fish scurry under the birds. I taught him the few spells my sisters had taught me. He would sit open-mouthed, eyes staring. But he never remembered. Or as storms broke the stillness, we would watch the white skies darken, the squalls coming in with a hiss like the waves. Such was my rule. In the gray cold mornings, when it would have seemed easier to have stayed in the hall, we would walk on the strand, throwing stones at the empty sea.

"Only one day we looked out and saw that all the wide sea was thick with sails, thicker than ever it had been with storm clouds or birds. The prows of the great ships pointed straight at the land. Men swarmed on the decks, shouted and lifted their spears. Like thunder their howls rolled across to us.

"The boy jumped up, his legs dancing with fear. We *must flee*, he cried to me. But, I thought, I have stood too long looking at nothing to be frightened when there is something to see. So I kept where I was; and the boy, though I had no power to help him, stood with me.

"We looked; and all at once up the slope of the beach a woman came toward us, out of the sea. The sheath she wore clung to her breasts and waist, nor did she free it for modesty but clambered up swiftly on the stones. A boy she had with her, scarcely more than a babe, his hair white with the morning as hers was black. But his shoulders were already big and in his hands he bore armor for two men. Never had I seen such armor. The new helms shone like twisting suns, the mail-coats gleamed. Yet, the god knows, the light in her gray black eyes was brighter still. She touched her brow.

"*Lady,* I called out joyously, *it is no great love I have for women, for my house is burdened with many, yet you I would gladly welcome*.

"Those deep eyes looked in mine. If I saw the warning there, the pride beyond all hope such as the *filidh* say the best men have when death is sure, yet I would not be warned. Her small breasts trembled in the cold. I longed to warm them.

"Tell me what you wish, I said, *for I see you have come in haste and not for nothing. Yet, though there is a fleet of fierce men at your back, if there is a thing that I might do and keep my honor, I will do it.*

"Her face was tilted up. Above the breakers I could hear the knock of warriors throwing down their oars.

"Lord, she pleaded, *if the mother of men put good in you, put on this armor.*

"Already the warriors were leaping onto the shore. Close at my heels the dog boy wept.

"Surely this is my death, I thought. Yet I would not die naked. *Only dress my boy as well*, I said, *for he stood with me when he might have ran.*

"So she helped me, and her white-haired lad moved with equal grace about poor Wyck so that we rose together, the shining metal braced and tight. It was the lad who put the helmet in my hand.

"Stand off, I said, *perhaps I may buy their mercy on you with my death.*

"But then he spoke, his voice colder and stranger than a child's. *It is against myself I've seen you armed*, he said. His eyes that were dark and unwinking looked in mind. *But not for this day. You must grow a little in wisdom and I in brawn before we meet.* As though to drive off the cold, he shook himself. He laughed then, deep as a man.

"Far safer were you by your sister's fire, he said. *There you would have had a lot more suited you; in your own bed you might have fathered kings. But you would watch the rolling deep.* His stern smile faded. I heard his breath. *It takes its price.* But before I found a word to answer he had turned.

"Slowly he went down among the stones to where the warriors waited. Seeing him, they cheered. A man came forward, a war chief by his crest and colors. He met the boy and, lifting him ceremoniously, carried him to the bow of the longboat pulled up farthest on the shore. At this there was a buzzing. Crowding around him, the warriors went into their boats.

"I rubbed my eyes. I said, *This will be my shame forever, that I stood staring while a boy came out of the sea and wished my death*.

"The woman watched me sidelong. But when she moved to back away, I took her arm. The flesh was cold but it was flesh, the small bones thin beneath. There was no glory. Like any of my sister's brats, she wriggled in my hand.

"*Woman*, I said, *what ill gift have you given me?* Her child's lip jutted out. I thought, For all her shining looks, she is no goddess but a maid. I held her tighter. She turned in anger and in one haughty glance took in the shore, the few bare fields, the pinched and cheerless town above. On the highest place my sister's hall lay cramped against the rock. Her eyes smiled spitefully. *Who will remember the landkings of this place?* she said. *It is the sea I give you*.

"*You gave me armor*—I scowled—*and my death, I think, though it was a boy who challenged me*.

"*He is my son*, she whispered. Then all at once her child's hurt face seemed changed again, burnt white against the sea. She was as she had been, a woman with a woman's loveliness. A patch of color climbed her throat. She moved against me. *My husband's gods reward you, lord*, she cried, *as I have gained only the hate of mine*. Her voice died in her. Her eyes had lifted to my face. I let her go. There was a silence.

"*It was because I am a woman that you took the armor*, she said at last. *We are not different. Because he was a man I took my own lord to my bed. Even as you, he knew not what he bought with that. For he has bound himself with oaths and will not remember what was always plain. And yet, though he will wreck the world, I gave a sword to him.* Her lips pulled back. *So I have armed you, lord, to stand beside him in his need, though he takes from me the one other thing that I have loved.* Her head was bent. I saw the tears that fell between her breasts. I might have spoken.

"Her mouth twitched a little, steadied. *He goes to kill my son.* She turned, looking up again. *And though he has arts and skills such as no man ever had, yet you must help him if you can.*

"I watched her blankly. I said, not understanding, *I am just a man.*

"*No man was given less than will be asked of him.* She smiled. From under the nightfall of her hair I saw, despite her sorrow, a kind of triumph in her eyes. She touched my neck. It was then she spoke the words that my poor dog boy will not remember, words fair and gentle as the summer dusk, as soft as sleep, yet warm they were as a woman's breath, the breath that wakes a tired man in his bed. I heard them and it seemed in answer my own blood burned. My head was dizzy. I seemed to fade. The firm flesh melted, steamed, and became a fog that, drifting, spread and swelled. My mouth grew long, my pale skin darkened, and my nails turned black. Unhinged from joints, my long legs widened and my back grew thick. I felt as though every part of me were moving until, against the armor, the metal split along its seams, splintered and, rooting in my flesh, rayed out as hair. So that when I had a shape once more to stand in front of her, it was a seal's.

"The boy was crouching at my feet. His face was twisted, the old lines gone and new ones rutted in their place. The wind came rushing coldly from the sea. Despite his silver coat, the new fat on his hams and thighs, he shivered.

"She smiled again. *The sea will never harm him, lord,* she said and laughed, *though I fear it will not warm him either.* She stretched herself and looked out at the waves.

"But my heart was filled with dread. *And what do you wish me?*

"*May you have peace, Glas Awyddn. I have no strength to send you out or call you back. It was yourself who promised me your aid. I did not ask it. Even now, if fear is greater than your pride, go back to your sister's house. By her fire you will find your man's flesh whole again.*"

His face, that was a man's face now, looked up. In the depths of his strange eyes I saw the memory of that cold shore, the memory of longing and pity: the man's longing for a maid, the pity, beyond all longing, that would not see her pain.

"So you swore the oath."

His chin rose proudly.

"Yet how did she know where I would be?"

Forcing his voice to steadiness, he said, "Lord, how could she know? She saw you only once. And, though she lay with you, she never knew your heart."

I stared.

Glas Awyddn's breath went out of him. His big hands shifted on his knees. "Lord," he said slowly, "how shall any living man come into being except a woman bring him from the womb? I cannot tell you what she did. It was not my plan or my contriving. Yet it was she who made me as I am."

His eyes met mine. "She sent me west," he said. "Twelve days across the slate-gray sea, west where nothing is but only fog and wind and rolling waves. Twelve days and we saw no men, no islands, heard no sound but the gull's cry, lost as we were, far from land. On the last day, when the sky was low and churning overhead, we saw your ship. Yet by the way it leaned and drifted, its sails unstrung, we did not think to find it manned. The day was closing. Weary, wanting only to ease the stiffness of our arms, we climbed onto the deck. Myself, I thought you were a corpse. It was my boy who rolled your head and touched your shoulder. Even then I did not wonder who you were. The thought of her so stirred me I could not think the lord that she would send me to would seem a man."

"Until I said my name."

"Lord, there were three you gave me."

"And none you knew."

"Let it be as you please," Glas Awyddn said.

But I shook my head. "Yet one you knew, though I would not say it."

His breath grew short and for a moment I could hear only the rain, the harsh pounding rain such as fell when with Tabak I left Morrigan. It hammered the deck and roiled the sea. So it falls, I thought, over the fields and the forests of earth, on the houses of men, the deafening rain that keeps away silence. So it may be that it fell on the gray roof stones of Tech Duinn, upon the House of the Dead. Glas Awyddn stood. "A sword she said she had given you with which to wreck the world."

We looked at one another.

"The name," I whispered. But though bravely he answered, I already knew.

III.
Old Men's Songs

8.

They have reason to love me in Hwawl, red Hwawl where in the blue of late evening the waters washed red on the shore. Upward from fish weirs the blood smell crept into the air, climbed out of the river like a mist. It stank in my nostrils. Still, I was king three years before I went to them. If they begrudged me this, I did not hear of it. Well enough they knew of my war with the barons. But when I had settled the matter at Dineiden, before the first snow, I went home. There I rebuilt the tomb they had raised up quickly to cover Yllvere. I had the rock quarried at Bheur and floated on barges. Because of the weight of the stone and the fear of ice, I had the barges refitted. The tax was heavy that year. Nonetheless, men thought, let him honor his dead. My strength was still new to them and the land once again was at peace.

The envoy from Hwawl came in the spring. I met him on the wharves, for his sail had been seen a mile upriver and word sent down to me. He was a big red-haired man of about my years. Already he had three sons, he told me, each the like of himself. Though none, he feared, would reach an age to have sons of his own. He looked down at his boots. The spring sunlight cooked his white face like a sausage. He sweated. So

one after another men came to me out of the towns.
From the cities it was always matters of land rights and
trade, and the bribes matched their purses in horses
and gold. Always I took what was offered, then did what
I pleased. But from the towns, from towns that were
too small for streets, from fishermen's cottages lost and
untraceable along the creeks of the saltmarsh, from huts
on the moorlands and the spare, scraped-up villages,
stony and comfortless under the white chalk hills, from
the least and the most forgotten of these came tales:
hounds that howled at noon and ate manflesh, boars
with tusks long as pikes, harts with two heads, giants
with none, green mists and leopards, demons, dead
men and dreams. In Hwawl, it was the Fuathan. Though
whether it was six or seven or only one who ranged by
himself up and down the rough banks, overturning
boats and grabbing with icy fingers at the legs of men,
he could not say.

The man had brought a girl with him, clear-skinned
and round-breasted, with hair red and disordered as
the flame on a torchhead. She was nearer fourteen than
twenty but had been well schooled and laughed when
she saw I was watching. How little, I thought, they
remember Ar Elon. Yet all things will be as they must.
He should have had me go with him without the gift of
the girl, myself and Glas Awyddn for company, though a
few soldiers with nets would have handled the matter
more swiftly and with less chance of harm.

Somewhere it is written what I did there, how I
hauled the river mage out on the rock, my ax sunk deep
in the slime of his chest. His hairsnakes tightened
around my neck; the coils spilled over my shoulders.
But against the puffed silver heads, pressed near my
mouth, I whispered my name. In terror they fled me,
sank back into the rushes and were no longer seen.
More than that I barely remember. For the space of a

few breaths there must have been silence, the silence of wonder, and afterward cheers. The sun winked in the branches, the water was spotted with shadows and flies. In the late, still afternoon I washed the gore from my arms. In the evening I was made a guest of the village.

Because they had no hall to hold us, the fires were built in the open. Under the boughs of a great rambling oak they piled up the wood, in the high solemn place closed off from the town where time out of mind their old men settled quarrels and the women told tales.

We climbed a steep embankment to reach it, away from the river, though the current's cool murmur kept in my hearing all the way through the trees. Above the wood, the land was scraped and cleared, the ground flattened by the long years the villagers had tramped there. Only the oak thrust upward, undiminished, indifferent to the stirrings of men. Undisturbed by their passing, by the bandy-legged priest, the dogs and the women, it breathed without bitterness. The sky, where only the tree reached, was quiet. No cloud hid the stars.

I had been the last to enter the circle. Before I had settled, an old woman hobbled in front of the fires. She was gap-toothed and ugly, her short arms greased to the elbows from skimming fat from the kettles. Some restlessness possessed her and she tugged at her rags, stamping her small feet impatiently until the last man looked up. The girl they had given me saw her and slipped her smooth hand in mine. The old woman chuckled.

"Well you have done for us this day," she cried, "though as well we have served you. For in Hwawl there never was a girl more likely to please. She is not so cold as Yllvere nor as fated as Géar, but will keep your side warm in the evening and in the cold of the morning deliver up sons."

I heard the men grumble. Whatever they knew of this, the name of the witch queen had filled them with dread. My eye opened wide. "Woman," I said, "where have you learned this?" I was thinking of Géar. But then the tables were being laid under the tree and the cooks came carrying platters and the boys bearing wine. We ate and the men laughed again. Their mouths crammed with meat, they recounted the terrors of the river mage, which grew in the telling. The young widows looked wistful and wept. Still they took the cups when the wine came around; with gulping sighs they drank their revenge. Some smiled after that. One, who had kept the boy coming, hiked her skirts to her belly and danced, her round legs red and stumbling in the light of the fires. The old wives scolded and howled, but the boys peered out from the branches and grinned. Once more the wine was passed. The priest hummed to himself; men put away sorrow. Warm talk and laughter filled the air. When the old woman stood, not a man shouted her down. The embers were dying and they were ready for tales.

She stood in the clearing, staring at where I sat on the high seat under the oak. She looked like a gray gnome of wood. Such figures the old ones placed at the feet of the dead—shrunken and quiet, watching with unwinking eyes the brief journeys of the living, the endless wearying voyages of the men who were gone.

"My lord," she said and held out her arms.

The feasting had ceased. The boys had climbed down from the branches and sat on the ground. A child had been wailing. Calmly, unhurried, his mother gave him her breast.

The old woman looked over the ranks of men, over the blank fields beyond them to the west. It may be, even before she spoke, that the listeners felt a vastness stirring, bodiless and invisible, over the farthest hills, the merest edge of a darkness, blacker than night. No breeze turned the leaves.

"In the West there is a tree...," she said and stopped, listening to her own small voice floating out on the silence. "A tree so huge that this great oak is but a stalk of grass beside it—so wide that in itself it is a wood. Yet never in the world's time had any man seen it. In secret, from one age to another, it grew. In its branches the great birds found refuge. Not the least of them was Badb, the crow that was Anu's. She made her nest at the summit, in the high place looking over the earth. And as vast as that tree was, so was the body of Badb. When she lifted her wings, a shadow covered the world, and the hills and the valleys fell into darkness all the way to the sea. In the harbors, thinking it was a storm in the mountains, the sailors hid under the decks, cursing the air. Only one man did not curse it or shake his fists at the darkness. He was a boy then and lived in the North, in a great house that women kept, keeping it and the boy to themselves. For they knew who he was, if he did not. They saw that if ever he lifted his eyes he would go out from their rooms, from their fires and their spinning, and the thing that he was, that they had kept and shielded out of longing and fear, that which they loved and had hated, would be free in the world. Yet one day, because it could not be otherwise, one day he left them, going up in the hills. And the wood that had always been closed opened up for him. In the darkness, under the roof of its branches, he found a stair...."

I lay back, hearing the voice of the woman, the tale moving in and out of my thoughts with my breath. My eye looked into the darkness. I remembered the climb and the fight I had with the crow. And every word the woman spoke was as I knew it. But a shadow crossed my face and I sighed. "Woman," I said, "surely you are

first among the tellers of tales. For although none came
with me, yet so clear is the telling you might have
climbed at my side. But long I have lived with this.
Tonight I would hear something new."

The men of Hwawl looked puzzled. *What tales are
more pleasing,* they wondered, *than tales of his youth?
What talk would he hear that is sweeter than praise?*
But the old woman smiled.

"If there were anything new, a king would have heard
it," she answered. But then she thought again and her
little eyes sank into her white withered face like knots
in wood. "Yet there are tales so old they are remembered only in sleep and never on waking. Such might
come new to your ears."

But Glas Awyddn glanced at her doubtfully. "Lord,"
he said boldly, "what is forgotten is best left where it
is." But I saw the men watching and stretched out my
hand.

"Would you had thought that," I whispered, "when
you gave me my name. Beyond that, where is there
harm? It is certain I never learned anything quickly. Yet
one thing is more certain: I never listened except I was
ready to hear."

He wore a man's face then as I did, the seal's
features wiped away, as though the years in the West
were but dreams that had troubled our sleep. It was a
man's bare face that stiffened. But I laughed and,
drawing a ring from my finger, I tossed it at the old
woman's feet.

Slowly she bent forward to grasp it. "Aye," she said
softly, both mocking and greedy, as a cat will take hold
of its prey, "as small even as this was the gift the Dagda
gave once to Ar Elon. . . ."

"An acorn?"

"A ship," I repeated, "for both were the same. The

long boards sprouted cold in the harbor. The walls by
the river blanched white with its shining and men hid
their eyes. So under the very spears of Thigg's soldiers
I left them, and the ship, though I had no skill with it,
brought me south to Tinkern and then onto Hren. But
when I saw the waves of the sea I despaired."

"My master can sail it," Wyck piped up bravely from
under my cloak.

Glas Awyddn sat quietly listening, his hand bent; I
could not see his face. The rain had been drawn up like
a garment gathered one fold after another to itself. The
water lay naked beneath it. I looked out. Over the bow
a few late stars glittered brightly. So the same stars
shone at the beginning, unfaded and close to the earth,
before men chased them away with their wondering.

"What is it you want?" said Glas Awyddn.

"What has any man wanted?"

The tall man looked up. "I should fear you, then," he
said.

"Fear a man?"

The wind made him squint. "Him more than the
Other."

Something scratched at the keel. Through the boards
I could feel it, though there was nothing to see. A long,
easy swell rolled under the ship, lifting it gently and
steadily, then setting it down.

"If there is land," I said, "I must find it."

"And if there is not?" said Glas Awyddn.

Wyck's mouth crooked up suddenly. He had been
waiting for morning. As he watched, the ship lurched
once more.

"We're aground," the boy whispered.

But there was no ground.

Behind, in the east, day crept above the edge of the
world. Glas Awyddn went aft in the new light to watch
it. Out of the shadows the sun lit his flesh like a torch.

"Lord," he said softly, "they have taken the sea."

I shifted under the awning. "Come quickly," he said. I went down to him slowly, watching the sky lighten, the sun grown huge and white off the stern. I stared out intently, glancing around and behind. But all I saw was ocean. The new sun poured over it, as pure and as clear as a spring.

Glas Awyddn shuddered. "Look into its depths," he said softly.

I looked down.

At first I saw nothing; and then, dawning on my eyes at no definite moment, I knew there were shapes, blurred shapes growing sharp in the dimness, shapes too massive and high for what should have been there. Crouching close to the rail, my mouth on the wood, I stared.

The face of the water was thinning. Soon there were mountains, their rough peaks thrust up and gleaming under the waves. Like a crow the ship slipped over ridges and walls, over heels of harsh stone half veiled in the flood, over bare slopes and hunched broken stone. Like the shadow of a cloud, the hull cast its long darkness over their backs.

Glas Awyddn caught hold of my arm. Leaning forward, he pointed.

Tugged by the wind, the ship drifted over a ledge. The rock ended suddenly on the brink of a cliff. On the far side, fallen steeply away, lay a broad open plain, a great bay cut out of the mountains and stretching west, league on league to the edge of sight. Clearing the peaks, the sunlight floated down to it, spreading out with its fingers. But the plain, when the sun reached it, was green, green with slow swaying boughs, green with bracken and sedge. There were meads and bogs and, though it was fathoms deep, the white shimmering thread of a stream, which passed out from the ledge

and wound under gentle hills and out onto the plain.
On the banks of the stream a house lifted its square
bulk against the green, jagged mass of trees. The smoke
from its chimney rose curling through the pale, shining
sea.

"There are men in this place," said Glas Awyddn.

"Not men," I said, "though, perhaps, if fires burn,
there is something to breathe."

"Indeed," said Glas Awyddn, "there is a way of
proving it." He moved up the deck. "Wyck," he said
sharply. The boy nodded. His small face looked calm,
but his eyes were glassy and his forehead was damp.
He backed off slowly, then turned, disappearing behind
the mast.

The ship scraped among reeds floating loose in the
sea. Squinting in the brightness, I saw low upon the
water a maze of tiny islets, hummocks choking with
marsh grass and the tangle of wet dwarf trees. The isles
glided past, following a spur of the mountain, curving
north and west at the edge of the plain. The waves
came in gently, sucking the weed. Glas Awyddn took
the steering oar, turning the ship in the current until it
slowed, nosing into a channel that skirted the margins
of a shallow hill. The breeze dropped in back of the
island. The ship, with barely a sound, drifted close to
the bank. The air was still. When the bow touched the
ground, Glas Awyddn went forward to see to the
mooring.

He came back with Wyck at his heels. Between them
they carried their armor, the boy struggling under the
weight of brigandine, the sleeve of the bright mail
caught firmly between his teeth to keep it from dragging. He marched along dutifully, steady and serious;
but now and again he glanced at Glas Awyddn, his
child's face red as fire. Glas Awyddn saw it. He laid
down his arms, searching out from the bundle a coarse

gray shirt to go under the rings and a belt set with silver.

The boy held his breath.

"You must stand by the rail," Glas Awyddn said lightly. "It is enough that one of us tries this."

Wyck made no answer, but took hold of the mail, lifting it high to the tall man's shoulders. The armholes were stiff; Glas Awyddn grunted. Even magic, I thought, has its flaws. I could not help thinking of Géar. Foreknowing, she had fashioned him armor; in whatever place she kept she had waited and watched, knowing the shape of the man she must meet, thinking, *This will be the girth of his waist, this the span of his shoulders*— though the man never stood in his flesh by her chair, never bowed his neck the least jot, never guided her hands. So, by small measures, she misjudged him; and the mail pulled tight and fell short at the wrists, and under the arms it was open.

His face was ablaze from the sun on the metal. The boy tugged the last buckle into its place. The man turned from him to look at the island.

A line of old alders grew close to the bank. Some of the cones, already fallen, bobbed swollen and black in the wash. Beyond, the hill and the trees were green, but it was the wild, late green of summer's end. It was winter, I knew, when I had taken my leave of Tech Duinn.

"You are a fool to come with me," I said.

Glas Awyddn smiled. "It cannot be helped." He passed his hand slowly along the finely wrought rings of his shirt. "Least of all can I help it. I was there when a woman came out of the sea."

He walked ahead quickly. At the bow he lifted himself over the gunwales and jumped to the beach.

All I saw for a moment was the hot sunlight glittering white on the shore. Presently he crossed into a shadow.

He lingered awhile, catching his breath in the coolness, then began to walk once more, moving away over the sharp gray stones. Just inside the point a great bare rock ran into the water. He leapt onto its back. By then he was well out of hearing. His hand came up slowly to his face. I could see he was whispering.

The change began at his feet. His head drew back once; a short, quivering wave passed over his neck. For a moment again he was motionless. The sun baked his fur.

A light breeze blew over the blazing mirror of the sea. I stretched myself out on the deck, listening to the water. The boy nodded sleepily. There was a bird in the alders. I could hear its sharp, bitter song. It kept me awake.

It was not a crow. Crows haunted the inland meadows, prancing on turf and walls, pecking in the stacks of dry hay, finding next to the byre the corpse of a badger left prickly and dead. A few, smaller but no less glossy and black, scavenged the channel islands. But there were none out at sea, none to perch on my shoulder or whisper a name.

Wyck woke and turned over, laying his dark head near my knee.

"She was a crow when it pleased her," I said.

The boy looked perplexed.

"The woman," I said, "who came out of the sea."

It was almost midday; the sky was empty and clear. The boy yawned and sat up, my cloak slipping off his shoulders.

"It must be soon," I said. "Get up and dress yourself in your armor."

He poked at his feet.

"Twelve days you lived in the sea," I reminded him.

He shivered and had to clench his teeth to keep

them from rattling. His eyes found my face. "It was Glas Awyddn who spoke to her," he said stiffly. Yet he stood. "Lord," he said over his shoulder, "I have lived on the sea, never under it." His lower lip trembled. Shamed, he looked out at the west.

All at once he shouted.

Even as I lurched to my feet Wyck ran to the rail. With a bound he was over it.

In the wide quiet bay I caught a glimpse of Glas Awyddn's head—his cheek gashed and swollen, his muzzle smeared with blood. He struggled to rise, but his strength went out of him, and he fell. Gentle waves scudded over his chest. He snarled, then flung out his hands, grabbing hold of the weed. The bird shrilled from the bluff. He turned his head, listening. His wide nostrils twitched. By then the boy had reached him, but the man waved him back. Glas Awyddn stood. When he waded ashore, grimy with blood and with weed, he was grinning.

"There are men," said Glas Awyddn, resting close to the fire Wyck had made for him. Stars frosted the blackness. Already the wind blew cold, but so near the fire my clothes reeked with sweat. I pulled myself back and sat under the trees. "At least there was one," Glas Awyddn said. He slumped back and sighed. "It was not long after I set out that I came to a river. Nonetheless, I was a good while walking beside it, for the current was swift and I saw no way to cross."

Wyck's eyes were wide. "Lord," he said softly, "how can there be rivers under the sea? Or, if there are—for you have gone there and seen one—how can there be any great trouble in crossing them?" He stared at the man, his face flushed in the light. "I"—he said swallowing—"I—I would have swum over its back, for the sea would be everywhere."

Glas Awyddn laughed. "There the water is thin. A man walks through it much as a man walks in the air. The wind blows, or what seems like wind, for the grass moves and whispers. And when I took my breath, what I breathed was both bitter and sweet, smelling of hay and pitch, the sharp smell of dung blowing down from the hills." He waited.

From the darkness outside the fire I watched him. "Go on," I said.

Glas Awyddn smiled wanly. "At first," he said, "where I walked, the land to either side of the river was open. But as the river slunk forward the grassy slopes gave way to bracken and then to a wood. Grim old trees hunched over the track. The long boughs were twisted; they scratched at the sun. Between the black roots the water rushed on over terraces, rank and slippery with weed, plunged thundering into pools, then fell away again in the dimness until even that great roaring was lost and quiet under the trees. I went on warily, keeping close to the bank. Now and again a chill light flickered between the boughs. For a moment it would speckle the mist and the stone. Then all at once something flashed in the river.

"Turning my head, I saw there was a man standing alone in the flood. He was leaning hard on his spear. At his waist a long sword was buckled. As I saw him he was lifting it free.

"His head was uncovered. For the rest he was well warded with ring mail and iron. But his sword and his armor were as red as his hair. Before I could speak he bowed low to me.

"*You are in dear straits, Glas Awyddn,*" he said. I looked and I saw him; and yet I felt a loneliness, deeper even than the loneliness of the wood, sucking close to my heart.

"The Redd Man watched me. *Unless I carry you,* he

said, *you cannot cross*. He was silent a little, then added: *Nor will I carry you unless you first give me the thing that I ask. For here is the only way into Tir fo Thuinn. Since the beginning no lord has ever gone in or gone out of it except with my leave.*

"For another space there was silence. Then I said quietly, *It will not be a small thing that you want.*

"*To some it is little.*

"*And to you?*

"*Have you loved?* said the Redd Man.

"I stood stiff on the bank. *Once*, I said softly, but the dread of that answer caught fast in my throat.

"The river was heaving. For a moment I could hear no sound but the water swirling against him. I stared but there was nothing to see.

"Yet, looking down from the ship, I had seen the green land that must lie beyond, a land brighter and greener than any land above the sea. I longed to run forward across the cold water, through the dark wood and out onto the green bright plain, under a sky like no other. It was such a place she had promised. For nothing less had she given me armor.

"*Tell me the price*, I said hotly.

"*No more than one drop of your heart's blood*, he answered, his voice just a whisper. I was not certain he spoke it aloud. Yet his lips moved. I saw the sweat of his brow. *Come then*, I murmured. *If you will have it, you will not have it idly.*

"*Nor did I mean to*, he said. And as he spoke he cast his great spear.

"The shaft whistled past me, with such force that the point halved the tough bole of an oak. The deep wood lay open and bled. When he saw where it struck, he sprang forward. I leapt down to meet him.

"The water hissed cold at my knees, came clawing and shouldering until it seemed bodies and arms. Heedless, the Redd Man plunged through them. He was waving his sword. By a hair's breadth I ducked him, my own blade coming up, flickering close to his head. Grunting, he knocked it aside.

"So for some minutes we drove at each other. Many cuts I had from him then, many rends and slashes, but nothing went deep. For as fiercely as he hurled himself at me, I hurled myself back. Yet as the day wore my lunges grew wilder. My head rang, dizzy and racing with blood. I felt my arm stiffen.

"Panting, I struggled out to the slab of a stone sticking out of the river, scrambled up on its sides to get my height over him. I was still but the shadows were running. The trees ran and the river was shrinking away. Even the darkness grew small. It quivered and shrank. And yet in that smallness I seemed even less. I turned my head sharply. He was waiting. His red hair lay wet on his neck.

"*You are a brave man, Glas Awyddn*, he said, *but a man's breath grows short*.

"With the last of my strength I struck out at his face. The metal beat only on emptiness.

"He was smiling. I saw, though I saw nothing clearly, the flash of his sword leaping high to my chest.

"I shook when it touched me as though a sliver of ice had been laid at my heart. The smooth flesh parted, just under the arm where the ring mail was short. A single drop slipped from the cut like a tear. On the hard edge of his thumb the man caught it.

"*It is little enough*, said the Redd Man, *yet it is all that I bargained*.

"But as suddenly my wits had come back.

"*What thing have you taken?* I said. *It is not my life, for I have it*.

"His gray eyes were gentle and sad. *There is*, he

said, *another thing that is gone with it. But come, for I owe you in turn.*

"*You are bound to it?*

"*Yes.*

"*Though I were twice what I am?*

"He nodded.

"*Or twice that again?*

"*Though you were a mountain,* he said, *I would carry you.*

"*Now?*

"*At your will. This bargain will keep.*"

Glas Awyddn grinned but his long face was pale.

"So I left him," he said, "climbed up toward the air, though then I was weary. On the shores of the high world I could scarcely make myself stand."

He shifted, drawing himself nearer the fire. "So I have earned our passage into the land. For if I grab hold of you and take Wyck as well to my side, he has sworn he must carry us.

"He has sworn," he said, staring in front of him. His gray lips were set in a smile. He was trembling.

"Lord," he said softly, "it is cold in the air."

I looked past him. Nor did I tell him then the thing he had lost.

9.

Of course it felt like going home; but then there never was a footpath that led wet to a hollow, a dry lane into Abereth or a paved street in Tyre I did not feel somehow was bringing me homeward. How then could it matter this flesh had not been there, never gone to those distant and invisible halls? Even the birds of one season, April spawn and untraveled, feel the same sweet longing in the blood. In the cool, shortening nights thickening into blackness, when the sand is quiet, before the storms pour eastward and the winds whirl loud across the dunes, the birds gather. Asleep, their short necks curled under their wings, they dream of countries that, waking, they have never crossed.

Not this meat. Little did Llugh know of that land, not his pale flesh that I wore, wore in truth before he had use of it. Yet the blood, born over and over, saw it clearly, saw without needing to look the morning lying flushed on the back of the sea, heard without listening the cool murmur, the cold endless rush of the tide as it fled over great bedded stones. Sharp as the sword of the Redd Man the memory went through me. I did not turn my head. In the cheerless halls of *Tir fo Thuinn*, the old men waited and sang.

Glas Awyddn shivered.

He was sitting on a small ledge of stone next to the fire, drinking from a cup of hot wine Wyck had given him. His lesser wounds had closed; the great wound had not. During the night the boy, who at last had struggled into his armor, had cleansed the broken flesh. With care he had dressed it. Before dawn I had watched him tearing strips from my cloak. Now he shook his hands above the wound to drive off the flies.

He said, "You must wait until it heals."

"No," Glas Awyddn said shortly and fell silent, gazing out with flat, vacant eyes. The water no longer reflected the land. The strong sunlight cut straight through the surface. Beneath the faint ripples he could see the green hillsides dropping away and beyond them, the deep vale of the wood.

The boy only looked at his feet. He had grown very red in the face.

I was not part of this and waited.

At last Glas Awyddn spoke, his voice roughened and grainy with weariness. But though weary, his breath was a rising wind. It blew over the body of the boy, bearing the words Wyck would never remember, words that tasted like blood, that slid like oil into the creases of his flesh and yet had no permanence. Shaming him, they slipped from his mind though already he had heard them, once on another shore, the woman rising cold from the sea, making no effort to hide her disdain for the land or to cover her nakedness. Her little dark nipples had pressed close to his chest. They boy's flesh moved. His ears ringing, he no longer heard.

The small, dark eyes never left Glas Awyddn's face. The young seal said nothing.

It was like walking out of a warm, hushed room into rain. We went single file, descending through a monotonous and persistent mist along the edge of an escarp-

ment, then down a deep cleft in the rock. Stones we
idly kicked aside tumbled slowly in the current and
tangled in weed. The narrow ravine turned and
plummeted. Carefully, edging our way, we climbed
down from the sky.

At the bottom the deep grass flourished and the
sorrel burst into damp purple bloom. The waves crawled
above us, casting long shadows below. At first we could
hear the dull thunder dragging over our heads. But
soon even that came to nothing. To the south there
were patches of brightness. Glas Awyddn walked ahead.
Some steps behind, we followed him. The mist died
away of itself. The ground seemed almost dry again.

Not a soul was to be seen; even the grass seemed
untrampled where earlier Glas Awyddn had walked to
the wood. The hillside was silent. I listened, hearing
only the stony noise of the river as we approached the
trees. The air was full of the scent of thistle and leaves.
The boy dawdled, dragging his heels, his thick feet—
not truly a man's nor a seal's—scratching tufts from the
grass. The late sun fell straight in his face. On his short
neck the fur stood out stiffly.

"You did not change," he complained to me in a low
voice.

A strand of my white hair had come loose from its
binding and covered my cheek. Without answering I
thrust it back.

The boy pushed out his lip resentfully. "I kept his
hounds," he said. "It was not so much. But he kept me
because there were hounds to keep—though there
were no more pigs in the wood to keep them for. But
the memory of the pigs was something." He glanced
sideways, avoiding my eyes. "He had no more than
that, only the memory of kings in a land where women
ruled."

"He has left that place," I said.

He dug at the grass. "Aye," he whispered. "*He* is something now." His breath came fiercely.

I turned his head. Above the bristling snout the eyes were dazed with grief. I looked down at them and into his face that was a boy's face still, from which the reshaping had neither altered nor worn the hunger or loneliness or the longing for glory. So ever it is that boys, before they are fit to stand, would be off, though the road never led elsewhere but to dying.

I raised my hand.

In the hall it brings no quiet.

"Had I another day," the old man pleads, dry-lipped, remembering the lost weight of his loins that for thirty years had been cold and lifeless, "*Had I another hour, lord, I would have kissed her.*"

I am not listening.

"I would also serve you, lord," he whispered. Softly, sorely, the boy had begun to weep. I too had been like him. I remembered that.

Small figures detach themselves from the throng and come across the floor to stand at my chair. The sweet, nauseating smell of burning flesh blows through the hall. A screaming woman wriggles at my feet. "It cannot be!" she rails, her hair in flames. "I sprinkled blood on the step, left milk for elves. Whenever I baked the bread, I blessed it, twice."

I look away.

"Lord?"

Because he dared no longer hope, I pitied him.

"Until the end of all things come," I said, "you will not serve me. Be what you will be, your heart will not lose its strength or your flesh fail. Only never let it be said I have no mercy. This one I have saved."

The boy watched me, uncomprehendingly, as though across a great space he watched the moon.

With my lifted hand I struck him. The seal shape

came apart, blew into a mist that wavered and became a shape again. Startled, he looked down at his hands and feet, running his eyes across his flesh. He drew a breath. And then another as though he were not yet certain the chest that filled was his. His head came up. His eyes burned.

Glas Awyddn's back was twisted; he favored his arm. Nonetheless, now and again, he stooped painfully, studying the ground. After several minutes he halted. Kneeling, he caught something between his webbed fingers, rubbed it twice, then brought it under his nostrils.

"There were soldiers here," he said, not looking around. "Not an hour past. Here they waited. Here one lay, though I fear he took but fitful rest. See, his wounds were many and he bled."

"Then they will not be far," Wyck said, a strangeness in his voice.

Glas Awyddn wheeled back toward him as he spoke. A boy's shape crowded suddenly into his sight. He made himself still. The field was silent. "We shall overtake them in the wood," Wyck said quietly. "Still, we shall make no haste ourselves, for your wound is deep."

Something changed in Glas Awyddn's jaw. "How came this?" he said.

But already Wyck was looking past him, his keen eyes following the path of the river. The light was dying. In the place where the river turned and vanished under the trees its icy waters glistened queerly.

"I will have an answer," Glas Awyddn said.

Wyck cocked his head. The air was darker. A thin wind stirred the grass and set it trembling. It carried the screams of a man.

"They will have met him," Wyck said grimly. Harsh

as crows the clang of weapons climbed the ashen sky above the wood.

The banks were fissured and eaten away by the current—a warren of holes and awkward overhanging rock. The water swirled invisibly beneath, ripping the low twigs from the bank and bearing them off with it. The air hung close. Rank and heavy, smelling of earth and sedge, it distorted the scrape of metal, the grunting of breath. His eyes glazed, Glas Awyddn stumbled ahead distrustfully. He shook his head, trying to clear it of weariness. He seemed uncertain of the way, though it was clear enough that all that was needed was to follow the river. The few stars that shone like cold sparks through the branches only deepened the gloom.

Glas Awyddn cursed. "I have not the wit to find it, lord," he said miserably. "In the day it seemed like night. But the night is blacker."

But the blackness blew cool on my neck. A joy washed over me. Such was the darkness underneath the hill, in the hall that was nearly finished. I looked around, remembering the endless room where no true fire ever reached. *Behold my court*, I thought. Though I saw nothing, its beauty was before me, there as it had been, remembered and dreamed, through all the years that were and those that would be. I smiled. The dead hosts murmured. Like the tremor of the sea against the stone their changing, intermingled voices melted into a roar. I lifted my own. Its greater sound swept forward over them, more splendid and terrible, like the voice of the storm.

Glas Awyddn was swearing.

I woke.

His shrill cries rose higher, drowning out the sound of the sea. He was lost.

Yet I knew the place well enough when I reached it.

The huddled shapes of the sealmen lay powerless, crouched in the shadows, in the ruin of the wood. Except for the fear in their faces they might have been stones. But the old man, leaning hard on his spear, stood out plainly.

"Good evening, Mug Dafad," I said to him.

"You have my welcome, lord," the Redd Man answered.

Glas Awyddn stared. His breath hissed painfully. "You knew him," he whispered. Fist clenched, betrayed, he was pressing near me.

"Be still," I ordered. "You did as you wished." In the grumbling echo of my voice I could hear the storm. The mist rose up from the river in curling threads.

His ring mail rusted and fouled, Mug Dafad waded toward the bank. Even in the darkness I could see the gore and weed that clung to him. Six-handed, like an ungainly spider, he crawled across the stones. His large bare feet were swollen. His horse teeth chattered. He made a face.

"I would have stood at a gate," he said glumly. "A gatesman at least has some dignity, a dry place to stand. You might have seen to it, in respect for my years. Not a gift, mind you. What I ask I have paid for. Earned, I should think, by those years underground, long years, though in truth I do not mourn them. . . ." He stopped. A moment's strange recognition wavered, passed over his eyes. "I have good cause to remember," he muttered, "for I had all my strength and outshone all men."

Grunting loudly, he made the last leap to the bank. Muck trailed from his armor.

"A gatesman would have been just," he scowled, glaring down at his thumbs, at the spots of blood on them. "I am no butcher."

From the tangled brush, hurt, the sealmen stared at him. Nicked and blunted, their swords lay out of reach.

"Who are they?" I said.

"Kings. Like you, Ar Elon's spawn." He met my eyes. "The god knows how many of the hundred isles Ar Elon bred on, how many women, clasping him, he left with sons. I doubt he counted."

My heart came to my throat. "You know this?"

But I saw he mocked me. Under his shaggy brows, his gray eyes smiled again. "Who is to say?" he answered. "Myself, I have given little thought to it. The work you set me lies the other side of birth. But surely as their toes are webbed, some sea thing got them and none but kings or those that follow them would brave this land."

"Or you," I answered him.

He laughed. "Lord, they gave me what I asked. At least I took it. So if they wish it still, with what is left, they are free to follow you."

The three lay motionless, one upon the other as though their wounds had stuck them there. I walked around them. Though the darkness smothered their faces, I could just make out the spikes of seahair, dark and light, uncoiled on their shoulders. The wind blew over them; but, if it gnawed their flesh, they were afraid to shiver. I pulled my sword and struck the nearest with the flat of it. The man looked up. His round eyes focused some distance to the left of where I stood.

"Can you stand?" I said.

He drew a breath but gave no greeting.

I turned my neck. "It is better," I said, "their land were left to women than to have such ill kings over them."

The man sat up. His face was vague as a web of shadows. He looked at the river.

He is gone, the man said wonderingly. The voice was distant, like the buzzing of a fly. I strained to hear it. Another shifted, kneeling, reaching with both hands for his sword. He moved without noise, his garments blurred.

The blade, half as long as himself, he jerked up suddenly before his face. The point, touching nothing, flicked past my knees.

Did you see him?

No. A darkness.

The third man rose, his long white hair unbound, brushing his tired face.

There are others, he said. *I have heard them whispering.*

The youngest looked very hard at the trees, at the partings between the gray branches where, in the sky that was under the sky of heaven, a darkness gathered. *Perhaps a storm is coming*, he said.

I would know thunder.

The youngest bent his head slightly. He could see the mist, tarnished, the color of smoke, lagging over the back of the river. *It is ghosts, then*, he said. Wyck was standing in front of him. Gently, as though he were touching a wound, he reached out his fingers.

"He has my own face," Wyck said steadily. But his voice stopped and he let his arm fall.

Through his white lashes the eyes of the pale king smiled. *Be at peace*, he said to the youngest. *Many heads would have rolled at his feet had he wished it, for from all the world's islands men come to him. Yet, had it been so, when we ourselves came to the ford, there would have been only their picked bones to walk on.* He turned his head silently. For a moment he met my gaze. For an instant he held it. As men watch the small stars flare cold in the dusk, so we watched one another. One by one the stars melted. He took the boy's arm. *No*, he said slowly, *there are corpses enough. What need has he to add to them?*

Glas Awyddn groaned, his eyes brooding on what could not be seen in the darkness. Men he saw, warlike and tall, and heard their hard voices: two black and grumbling as seals; two pale as the wave's crest, guileful and whispering; one red—even as night flooded over him—as blood. Among them he saw his own face but joyless he turned from it. Once he had seen her; in awe he had watched her climbing wet from the sea. But now, when he tried to remember her, he could not. Even then he could not imagine a world with her gone from it. Yet it seemed, so violent was the pain he had, that there was only wind and emptiness in the place where he had kept her memory.

"He knows," Mug Dafad said softly.

My own face, white as one star in the darkness, was still. "We shall cross then," I said. "In truth he has paid for it."

The hard, ageless strength of his arms locked hold of my flesh. I felt his great hand on me, unexpectedly gentle—his old hand, sticky with blood. With five other hands he groped for the rest. Then, unfaltering, though the storm screamed over us, he bore us into the flood.

The darkness on the other side was full of trees, thrashing in the wind and rain. The downpour brawled. Leaning forward, Mug Dafad set me at last in the shallows. Men splashed around him, skidded and swore, getting their legs in his way. A thing swerved past me, as dreams pass—a thrust of air, flashed across my sight and gone. Unmindful, I slogged up the bank, turned, and glanced behind to make certain that the others followed. The ground was rutted. It fell away in soggy clumps. Sunk to his knees, Wyck tried to stand. Pitching forward, he scrambled, seized a slippery root, and hauled himself exhausted on a stone. Glas Awyddn labored after him, his teeth bared in a wretched grin. His limbs were shaking. I caught him by the shoulders; and, his weight against me, led him up the bank. I

propped his sagging back as best I could against a tree.
He moved to raise himself.

"Lie still," I ordered.

He looked down dolefully.

The three were gone. For the space of several breaths
I listened. I could not be certain. It was, I knew, no loss
to me if they had vanished. For, seeing his other lives,
what man would follow me? Surely a man would think
on it. Not Glas Awyddn perhaps. What had he to think
on for the moment but his pain? I waited for Wyck to
speak. But he only sat, his rank clothes sodden, a
stream of water dripping from his hair.

Thunder cracked above the trees. Mug Dafad, his
back to me, waded again into the river. In the murk it
was hard to see, and yet I watched him go, unbidden,
already out of hearing, to the place I had set for him.
For all his mockery, alone he served me faithfully.

There is a scent—like bristling smoke—of wool. I
smell them before they cross the threshold. I have
ordered the doors of the winter hall left open despite
the cold. They will see they are expected, know whatever lies are whispered, that they have not caught me
unprepared in this. Great-shouldered, weighted with
silver, they walk unhurried along the line of empty
tables and the sprawl of stools. The old woman, rising
from her corner, stands forth to announce them. With a
glance at one another, to test me, they wave her back.
They think my heart will stop before their stares. But I
know each one of them and could, if they would ask it,
name the man who dyed the wool of their rich mantles—
for I know the color—and even the village, east of Tyre,
above the seawall where the loom was kept, and—the
god knows—the woman, her white arms lifted, who did
the work.

The hangings to either side of me flap in the wind. In the yard I hear their soldiers. For the rest, with all my housethralls fled, the hall is quiet.

"You are early," I say to them, "and in the wrong place."

The barons scowl. Inside the wool their flesh is lathered with sweat. They have ridden the best part of a week to stand here, whipping their horses, driving men and beasts over the icy hills from Reddmarch, so great is their eagerness.

The seahair has fallen loose from my shoulders; the green ragged edge of it covers the twisted gold of the hilt. The sword is spread on my knees. I will not move to touch it. I say, "Not until spring shall I summon your armies. And then I shall lead them myself, at Tywy." Hring breathes something inaudible. He thinks I should tremble. He is a man without luck. At Dineiden, when I slaughtered the barons, he groveled and squealed. It was on that wide field with all his men pushing up from behind, staring, when with red, sweating hands he grabbed hold of my cloak. Since I spared him he has never forgiven me.

"He comes from the sea," I say to him, picking him out from the rest. "Out of *Tir fo Thuinn* with a thousand ships. And not a man with him has ever stood on the land." I look around calmly. "They have webs for toes. In their clawed hands they wield tridents instead of spears." I pause. "If we let them," I say, "they will fight in the surf." There is no anger in my eye, only false weariness at their misreckoning. "Did you think that on the dry streets of Ormkill I would have need of you?"

Hring's face is swollen with rage. "In the god's name," he shouts at me, "why do you think we have come?"

Unn has stood so quietly by my chair they have not guessed she is weeping. Her hand slips from her mouth.

"Who will meet those fell ships if you murder him?" she wails.

"It is only the king he wants," says Anhils stubbornly. He is second to Hring, keeping a step back in his shadow. One of his hands is hidden in the thick of his mantle.

They are only men and cannot imagine how I long for death.

"Let your men come to me," I say. "Lest there be any lies said of this, let it be in their sight."

At the doors the captains have watched. When Hring nods his assent, they come forward, passing through the portal, blinking and uncertain, out of the cold sunlight, into the vast, darkened cold of the hall. A host of men push in after them, men who have been called forth from the warmth of their houses for winter soldiering. Their boots filled with straw, they have marched numbly over the frosted moors. Cursing the cold that comes down from heaven, they have come to see the death of the king. Through the dimness comes the scrape of their swords.

My flesh is yellowed and blistered and rots in the air. It accepts the knife blandly. It is done so quickly not even the queen cries out. Anhils is the first to see there is no wound. He holds the long knife stupidly. For a moment I think he will drive it in once more, not out of hate, but, like a child, in wonder. He cannot have listened when my harpers sang of my meeting with the men of Tywy. It may be it was only lies to him. Who is to say? That other time the men of the holding scrambled, breathless, back against the doors. They crowd me now.

I stand.

Despite the sea tusks and the stench of flesh, the

shape of my young manhood warms my face. I think of
the shining beach where I first came to land. The
western shore is lovely in April. Landward there are
clear green hills that mount, free of the sea's confusion,
as though by counted, separate steps toward heaven. A
girl is sitting on the sand. Through the bright austerity
of air I see her plainly.

"At Tywy," I say to them, "in the spring."

It is with one voice they answer.

The midmorning sun was cool, the light half-shaded
though we had left the wood and wandered the deep
grassland west of the river. The plain stretched off into
a haze, blue-green like the grass and purple at its
farthest edge. Wyck ran before us, his gloom cast off,
eager to see what this world held. I was left to tramp
beside Glas Awyddn. Because of his wound I was afraid
to urge him on. His fingers lingered near his side,
exploring the air above it. Yet something had hardened
in his stare. He craned his neck to look ahead.

Nearly invisible against the hillside, a great horse
tossed its head and whinnied. Another answered. But it
was only when it had trotted to the crest, its vigorous
strong shoulders and pale mane streaming against the
open sky, that I saw it.

Wyck halted, pointed toward the hill, and yelled.
"The green mares!" he cried, astonished. At once he
started off again, clicking his tongue and whistling as
though the beasts were nothing stranger than his hounds
or that, hearing his commotion, they might come to
him.

Glas Awyddn gave me a look across his shoulder. "In
this place how are there mares?" he said.

"You took the wound." I felt the creases deepen

between my brows. I said, "He will see the difference if
he gets near enough."

Glas Awyddn followed Wyck's progress up the slope.
"They will kick his head in for his pains," he said.

"No doubt that will be near enough."

I think he smiled. His heavy eyelids flickered. For a
moment.

"Listen," he whispered.

The two green stallions grazed the hilltop, pulling
the clumps of weed noisily. Wyck was already halfway
up, whistling and slapping at his thighs.

Instantly there came the din of furious galloping. A
wave of fur caps and faces broke at once above the hill,
reared in a prodigious rush, and, braying, fell upon the
startled horses. A dozen ropes uncoiled, flew. They
struck like snakes, catching the bare green necks, tangling the kicking legs, and held. Even then one stallion
stood straight up, shrieking like a man, wrenching the
ropes that bound him. He thrust his head, turned, and
sprang away. But as suddenly the sealmen were in front
of him. On the eastern spur of the hill, hobbled, trying
to catch the snares between his teeth, he fell. With a
howl of victory the sealmen slid from their mounts and
met him on the ground. The stallion snorted, trying to
evade the rough touch of the man who stroked his
neck.

"That was too easy," the sealman said. He grasped
the long mane disappointedly. "I'll wager he's been
caught before and tamed." His voice was loud. I heard
it clearly, booming over the beaten grass. He straightened himself, wiping the horse sweat from his palms.
The pale sun shone on the brown of his cheeks, the
blackness of his eyes. The damp length of his seal-hair
clung to his neck.

There were twenty sealmen with him, none quite so
tall, but like him, webbed and shining-haired, men lean

and brown as oak leaves, well muscled and vigorous.
They milled about the hill, walking around the stallions, examining the horseflesh with steady, piercing
eyes. There were no grooms. All seemed of equal age
and rank, young lords like those in the old tale whom
Ossary, King of Sciath, once took in fosterage, requiring
as a pledge of loyalty the sons of one year from each
tuath, from the defiant vassals who long had warred
with him. Indeed, the sealmen looked and moved as
though they had come to manhood in one house and
shared its purpose. In the tale—if I have not forgotten
it—when they had learned the use of arms, they killed
Sciath's king and burned the hall he had reared them
in. Who is to say? The old tales always closed with
death.

Glas Awyddn plucked at my arm. "They come to
meet us, lord," he said.

Already Wyck was deep in the press of men, but if he
were aware of them he gave no sign of it. He strode
forward, his body anticipating and sidestepping each
knot of men and yet not meeting any face. They saw, as
he passed them, the fevered expectancy in his eyes. He
went straight for the stallions. The sealmen let him go.
It was a sight worth seeing.

"He has always lived with beasts," Glas Awyddn said.

The first line of sealmen closed with us. At their head
the man who had been first to reach the stallion unbelted
his long sword and swept it up to touch his forehead.

"The White!" he cried. His huge face broke out in a
wide grin. The men jostling up behind him cheered. I
saw the faces turned to me. So, thinking I had won a
great victory, the men of Ormkill had turned to me
when I had come from the Mound, small men standing
with their swords unbloodied, thinking I had slaughtered
the hag, had spread the vile old wreckage of her flesh
across the hill. The pale sun glowed on their brown

faces. Someone shouted. But the memory, lying cold across my thoughts, remained.

The first stepped up to me. "Lord," he announced in a loud voice, "you are a better sight than all the sea's horses. Truly, we had wearied of listening to the Penandrun tell of your coming. Too long they have been here. They can never remember whether it was once you came or whether you were yet to come." He clapped his webbed hand on my shoulder. "But that you are here is clear enough." He gave a great laugh.

"Llugh!" a man cried. And the host of sealmen answered: "Llugh-Llugh-Llugh."

The grass was thick on the hillside. The sealmen had come down from the place where the stallions were roped and hobbled, leaving Wyck alone with them. Leaning over a broad green back, he twisted its mane in his fingers. Vague transparent clouds drifted across the wide sky. His thin chest swelled with a breath. For no reason, merely for the stillness of the morning and the strength of the powerful beast under him, Wyck smiled.

"I shall walk," I said. The sealman who had brought me the harnessed stallion gave it instead into Wyck's hands. Very small Wyck looked beside it. Yet he patted its flank and though they had no horses in Tir na Trí Oileán, he threw his narrow legs over its back. He clicked his tongue loudly. The stallion took two quick strides, then halted, twisting its head to look at him. Wyck laughed and drove his fingers beneath the mane.

"You will make a good horseman," the sealman said.

"Who would not, upon such a beast?" Wyck answered. He was still smiling, his eyes spellbound with cheerfulness.

Two men were needed to lift Glas Awyddn up behind

a rider. Because he had little strength in his arms, he was bound with three bands of leather. Nonetheless, he held himself straight and, when it seemed to him no one was watching, out of pride he loosened the straps.

Once more the sealman brought me the reins. His eyes were alive with curiosity tinged with uneasiness. All the rest had mounted. I shook my head.

"Lord, as you will," he said and, bowing under my gaze, went off to find his own place in the troop. I knew I would slow their going, but there were few beasts that could bear me, even the brawny green stallions of the Penandrun's plain. I recalled the great bay I had ridden from Morrigan, thieving it from the stables while the women slept. I was still a boy then, though none could have told me that. Already I had twice the height of the men I knew.

For the first time I spoke to them:

"Your horses are for children."

The sealmen were quiet. They went slowly so I could keep their pace.

High in the upper air, where the sky seemed sea again, there were dolphins. Like shuttles they wove their dark bodies before the sun's diminished face, crossing and recrossing above the horizon. The light met no other obstacle. It flooded the endless grassland with a glorious enrapturing green, richer and more luminous than any that grew on land. However, it seems, I thought, it is grass. Still I did not look down often.

The track they followed was no clear road but rather a chain of landmarks: a hill with a certain slant, a forking stream; a grove of slight, green alders spied for a moment far up against the valley wall. It went mostly south. After two hours' walk, the sun moved at my back. Because they rode, we went without stopping. Beneath their fur caps the faces of the sealmen wore a chastened silence, the ruin of that eagerness which had brightened them when they had shouted the name they thought was mine.

The lead man brooded. The seal blood showed in him, in the tangle of his sea-black hair and blunt black eyes. His mouth was wide and grim beneath his bristles, not a mouth that was apt to stay quiet. His brown cheeks reddened. No longer able to contain himself, he threw aside his reins and dropped down beside me, letting the stallion trot along at his heels.

"I'd not tell you what to think," he said. "You are here to be lord of us. Yet what joy do we have but our horses?"

Though the narrow slits of their eyes were turned elsewhere, the sealmen listened. A murmur went through them, like a sigh.

He studied my face, staring longest at the ash-white hair that fell away from my forehead and covered my neck. "Since we came to this land," he said, "whenever the Penandrun give us leave from their chambers, we ride. They would teach us war, but it is only old tales they care for. It is better to ride—better to cast a lance at full gallop, to take a head leaning down from a proud stallion's back. That is study enough." He swore, his mouth turning sourly. The burn on his face seemed to deepen. "By the god," he snapped, "what are the tales of dead kings to us?"

"It was dead kings who made this war," I said.

He scowled. "Such kings, however royal, will not fight it."

I let a moment pass, long enough so that he felt the silence.

"It will be fought," I said, "by men who swear to me."

He shifted. "I have sworn," he answered. His voice

was guarded. Yet, like the sound of stones struck in the sea, it carried.

The wind roused. Smelling of horses, it blew southward over our backs. The sealmen pressed nearer, looking elsewhere, and listening. Now and again one turned his head. Something seemed to hover, mothlike, on the edge of sight. Men stared. There was nothing.

"When strangers come," I said, "who meets them?"

"No one. Or, by chance, as you were met, by men out riding. More often they find their own way in. It is a broad land, but there is nothing in it but the old one's court and the town around it. If any will brave the Redd Man, they will not be frightened by a little walk. They find us."

"And were you met?" I said.

"I wandered."

"How long?"

He gave a thought to it. "A week," he said, "or a season." He paused, glancing distractedly at the sun that was close to setting. "There is only day and night. And the days are like all other days and each night is the same." He looked, lifting his head, as though he had suddenly discovered a thing of worth was gone. "On land," he said, "I had twelve captains under me and knew each one and the year and the season each had sworn to me and the number of men he brought, even to the count of arrows their quivers held." He moved abruptly, a new thought breaking through the odd, preoccupied expression in his eyes. "I am Eachanhagen. Lord, I tell you that you may remember it. Almost I had forgotten. Hearing the old tales over and over, sometimes I mistake the old names for my own." His voice sounded husky. "We grow like them, those old men, forgetting our own names or how the days go or the season."

"So a man may cross," I said, "and wander some time before he is found?"

"Yes," Eachanhagen said softly. "So I have myself."

"Some days."

"Many days. Yes, or a season. It may have been a summer I walked this land."

"But in the end he is found."

He nodded. "Or he comes in himself."

"The Penandrun will not come out for him?" I said.

He spat. "They are where they are. As the sea is where it is."

Something swayed against me. I moved away from it. The sealman behind me wrenched his reins, avoiding the further touch of nothing he could see. The lines of horses broke into a strange confusion. I did not share it.

"Lend me the horse, Eachanhagen," I said. "Though it is small and unworthy, I've a mind to ride into the old men's town."

We rode, but the tracks of the horses were obliterated. They vanished with our passing as though the hooves were weightless, the deep marks worn away at once like muddy scrapings in the wellhead of a spring. Within a breath of our passing the *liobhagnach*, the sweet-scented weed that abounded in the valleys and on the low sides of the ridges, grew over the tracks. As swiftly as a stallion could gallop, so swiftly the *liobhagnach* healed. And when we were gone there was nothing to see but a featureless carpet of grass. And nothing for a man, though he looked with care, to follow.

The sky showed the first hint of twilight. The stallion bearing Glas Awyddn had to be kicked repeatedly to keep its head up and away from the weed. Yet the rider showed no resentment and the stallion paid him no heed. The troop moved slowly. Gradually Eachanhagen's gaze turned southward, traveling over the graying plain

as a sailor looks over water, its deep reflection darkening
the flesh under his eyes. A slip of a moon had risen
above the horizon. The horses passed along the ridge.
Soon they were only shadows, stubborn and black
against the sky's gentleness. Had there been watchers,
they could not have been certain whether they saw any
breathing thing but rather a grove of distant trees that
wavered a little and fluttered in the wind. Indeed they
must have been trees, for at last they rooted, and were
still in the darkness. Then, no watcher, even one who
looked with more than mortal sight, would have thought
it worth his while to pause on his journey or to climb
the steep bank to look at them.

The sealmen sat on the ground, resting against their
saddles, as though the smooth hard leather were the
softest of chairs, as fine as any Sciath's king set before
his fosterlings. The men had drawn off their caps and
sat waiting. Not a man among them had forgotten
courtesy. When we had eaten, without urging, they
gave me their names.

"Gwyn I was, Nudd's heir though I had no father,"
said a youth, his face high in the cheekbones, a thatch
of raven hair hanging down to his shoulders. "We had a
farm at Blaensawde. But early Nudd sent me away, up
the long valley to the shores of a lake to graze his cattle.
I went because he bade me but more I went, because
by the fire I had heard the women whisper that I was
the son of the lakeman. And, truly, I had not been
there long when I saw a tall old man sitting on the
surface of the lake. *Come then, Black One,* I cried in a
great voice. *Arise and own me.* As I shouted, the man
came walking across the smooth water. And when he
came to the shore he gave me three smart blows, and
not one of them was pleasant. With the first I laughed
bitterly and with the second I wept. But with the third
my thoughts clouded. Then it was a seal's head I threw

back and it was with a seal's clumsiness I lumbered into the lake to cool the itching of my skin. Thereafter I no longer walked on the land but hunted eels off the bank in the fogs of the morning. When autumn came, I found the river and went down to the sea."

I heard his breath, labored and puffing.

"You were Gywn," I said.

"Himself," said the youth. He set his two long-fingered hands on his knees, hands not only large but of extraordinary strength, with harsh round knuckles and blunt nails. Between the long fingers stretched a hair-less oily web. In the little light the moon gave, the dark flesh glittered.

Another raised his voice. "I was Dwfen," he said, "but though I lived below Cefyn Clun Tyno, on the sides of the mountain, with me it was much the same. For I left the house where I was fostered and went seeking my father. Still, I had not gone farther than the stream at the foot of the mountain when three men met me. And each one gave me a blow. When they had finished, the first went away with my sword and the second with my cloak and kirtle. But the third, pitying my nakedness, gave me a ragged brown skin to wrap around me. But when he saw me put it on, he wept. *My child! O My child!* he cried to me. *How shall you live on the land?* Hearing him, I looked down and saw the oily leather, my great feet splayed and widened like a seal's. So I hid myself, slipping away into the stream. Shamed, I sank beneath the curling weed into the cool darkness, out of the light, down where the current ran deepest, ran cold to the sea."

Lost in the memory, his fingers twisted in the lengths of his hair.

"And as well you were a fosterling?" I asked.

"I have said it."

"And each man here?"

Eachanhagen leaned hard on his saddle, his thick brows crooked up anxiously. Such ignorance was beyond his imagining. Unbelieving, he pushed close to my ear. "Lord," he whispered, "what he says is true. More, it is his honor. So he traces his blood to the seafolk and to such as would claim kin with you." He shook his head. His face was scarred with wounds. I could see the old hurts in it. "Why do you question them?" he murmured. "They are men and mean to follow you."

Beyond him, above the thrusts and folds of hills, the few stars blurred. The sea's chill breath eased nearer the ground, spilling its coldness over us. I held his eye. "It was yourself who said I could not trust your memory."

"Only the names," he said darkly, keeping a check on his anger. "In the years that have come and gone, many a man has had use of them. What lasting good, then, are our names to us? It is our deeds that matter." His voice was low; the sound of another rode over it, the gruff voice loud as it was filled with tenderness.

"South of the point at Fawkes," another youth began. "A furlong or so from land, the bay being still . . ."

Remembering, he covered his eyes with his blunt fingers. His voice rose and fell.

"Lord, my name was Annwn. I had a wife, although I can no longer see her face. . . ."

I looked into the dark, into the night shaping and reshaping itself as he spoke. His long memory ran before me. In the wet darkness, the few stars blazed and dwindled and blazed again.

I sat up on the ground. The rim of the sun had floated above the steep valley wall. The high sea crawled against the peaks. Its far sound came down to me. A dull thunder rolled over the plain. I pulled myself up. A knot of sealmen, already mounted, sat on their

horses, gazing impatiently over the ground. Eachanhagen
came to me, leading a stallion.

"Will you ride again?" he said.

I tried to remember whether I had heard his voice
among the rest. There had been many tales. In the end
I had lost track of the faces.

"Well?" he asked again.

I found the stirrup.

We left the place. Later, glancing back, I could not
tell that hill from any other. To the west and south lay
other hills, fair and green, waist-high with *liobhagnach*,
and no different from the ones behind. Like men going
watchful into the surf, the horses waded deep into the
weed. They moved at a slow trot, no distance between
them, as though they feared the grass had hidden
faults. Indeed, the horses sometimes veered at what
seemed nothing. Wheeling in one adhering mass, their
strides unbroken, they pulled suddenly to the left or
right and then plunged on.

A shiver of terror would run the length of my stallion. With ignorant reassurance I scratched his coat. He
tossed his head, whickering gently as though I had
earned his trust. But for myself, I was quiet, listening
to fragments of the sealmen's talk, their laughter sharp
against the hollow booming of the upper sea. They
spoke only of horses. I did not think. The mountains'
ragged rim fell far behind.

We went more quickly then, riding over the backs of
the hills where the ground was harder. Yet now and
then I heard the noise of water. Small streams washed
the slopes. Springs with hovering clouds of fog lurked
in the glens. Beside them dwarf trees bloomed, their
brief white flowers pale and small. In time I felt the
wind again. Grown cool and restless, its long breath
muttered.

Once in a sheltering valley, open to the south, I saw

what seemed to be a gleaming pillar looming tall in front of us. Its sides were crystal, flashing like the dew beneath the morning sun. But when we came nearer and could hear its roar, I saw it was a vast fountain, filling up the space between the land and sky. The ground shook under it. The air above was heavy and bent the light. It almost seemed the hills had broken loose, that they slid and floated over us. Blobs of weed, shining like bubbles, drifted upward. A cold rain drenched my hair.

"Even here," Eachanhagen shouted, "there are places where the land still wars against the sea."

"And which will be master?" I asked him.

He stared. A glistening runnel washed the side of his nose. But then he laughed. "One thing is sure," he boomed, "it will be fought in earnest now that you are home again."

We rode six days or seven. I am not certain. Far away to the south the land was rising. Wyck sniffed the air. He had taken to riding with a whip between his teeth. During the long hours of daylight he seldom paused. He cantered across the green meadows, moving easily in and out of ranks of the sealmen or standing, his full weight on the stirrups, he raced the clouds southward until we barely had sight of him. In the cool sunlight of the late afternoon, his pace slackened but, still without weariness, he leaned over the neck of the stallion, whispering. He had plaited his own thick hair into braids. He had done the same with the mane of his stallion. In the evenings he slept apart, the beast tethered near him where, if he woke, he could look at it.

Glas Awyddn stayed at my left hand. His face set, wasted by sickness, he did not seem to hear the hooves that pounded under him. His movements grew heavier and more blundering. Yet he would take no help. One

morning he would no longer let them strap him to his
mount. Exhaustion lay like weights on both his eyelids.
Cursing, his features disfigured, he tried to throw the
leather bands into the face of the man who had come to
assist him. The bands fell short. When he turned, I saw
the red stain wetting the rings of his armor. He wavered.

I caught him under the ribs.

"I can count his bones," I said wonderingly. Eachanhagen came trotting back along the line to look at us.
"How long before we find the old one's court?" I said.

"For what purpose?" he asked. "They have no healing."

"There must be somewhere."

He looked discomfited. "I will take you," he said
grudgingly. The sealmen behind him examined the
ground. Not a man looked up.

"How far?" I asked.

It was on the fourth day, at the close of it, that we
reached the house.

The dusk was already falling when we saw the first
trees. A pale glow lingered over the west, like airy
mountains—the faint double image of the more solid
peaks beneath. The land climbed steeply, rose, and was
broken into rough, uneven hills, their deep, grass-clad
backs turned gray in the twilight. Knots of low, spreading junipers clung to the banks. Farther off, dark,
columnar cedars huddled together on a hill, still as tall
old men. Eachanhagen slackened his pace. We had
descended into the fold of a valley and begun to mount
the ridge that climbed from it. Here the trees stood
nearer, like an army that had taken the land by stealth,
drawn up silently rank by rank across the valley's rim.
The sealmen looked up at the huge old branches doubtfully and rode closer together. In the cold air I could
hear the neighing of horses.

Beneath the tangled roots there were paving stones.
Sometimes I heard the nervous click of hooves against

them. Yet, if there were a road, in time we wandered
from it. Even then, in the gloom and darkness, I felt I
knew the place—though in truth it was not much like
the mountain wood at Morrigan or the trees on Hren.
Still, there was the same queer sad feeling of oldness,
like the air in a closed-up room where a man is dying,
where out of deference not a chair is moved. There was
no wind. If the moon sailed over the trees, not a flicker
of light slipped through the branches. So I had no way
of knowing how we found the house. Only suddenly
there was a wall that barred our way. We dismounted.
With fumbling hands I chanced upon a pair of iron
rings and fastened the reins. Someone had discovered
the door and knocked upon it. As the door was opened,
a shaft of yellow light flashed over us. Wyck stood in the
midst of it, his proud head bent beneath the low stone
lintel, his sword drawn and catching the light.

"Begone," a clear voice said. "Little enough peace I
have had from the sealmen. Little more will I get from
them."

"Whatever you grieve for was none of my doing,"
Wyck answered. He had lifted his blade and returned it
again to its sheath. At the edge of the light the sealmen
stared at him wonderingly. Quickly he spoke, but his
voice was soft and secret. Not a man heard what he
said. But neither did any man lean forward to listen for
each had turned from the door. So Eachanhagen turned,
his broad back to the house, gazing away from its
brightness.

"May he find healing," he whispered tonelessly.

With none to help me I took Glas Awyddn down from
the stallion. His eyes were clamped shut; in the gleam
of dusty light they seemed hollow. His dark head
sagged forward, his jaw coming to rest on my shoulder.
He was light as a child when I lifted him.

"Come," a voice said, "*he* is welcome."

I stepped over the threshold, tilting my head, turning sideways, pulling the thin legs of Glas Awyddn after me.

The room was large. In the hearthwall a great fire reached and shifted. But though I looked, I could not see into the corners. I turned. Even shut behind walls I made out the scent of grass, of bark and water, each vivid as though I had never entered a house. My nostrils quivered. From further off another scent came wafting toward me, slighter, masked beneath the cool smell of the evening, a scent so parched and wizened at first I barely noticed it. I let Glas Awyddn slip down by my waist and then down to the wide floor strewn with rushes.

"Leave him now," a voice behind me said.

A shadow came away from the door, walked slowly on the edge of the light, paying no heed to me. It stopped by the shape of Glas Awyddn, gazing down at him. A loose gown, falling straight from the shoulders and sweeping the floor, hid the tall figure. But with the cowl drawn back I saw the withered majesty of the face. Against the moving flames the straight long hair shone with a flinty gleam. The woman was old but with that strength that once in a great while time yields to age, as the fairest of metals is made pure by the fire. Unhurried, she removed a small knife from her gown. Spreading her slender fingers, she knelt above the body of the man.

Even in his swoon Glas Awyddn felt it. His eyelids fluttered, and for a moment his bewilderment was stronger than his pain. He had groaned.

"How . . . in this place," he murmured, ". . . are there women?"

A frown half troubled her face. "It is because I am old," she answered, mocking him gently. "The old are not women. So I am permitted. As well, when I can be persuaded, I do the sealmen some service." She leaned over him, her gray hair straying over the rims of her direct, unchanging eyes. Watching her, he was slow to see the knife. She rubbed it absently against a leather strap to sharpen the edge.

His brows flickered up.

The old woman smiled. "Be at peace, woman's child," she said softly. "No man can change what must come. The first wound you have had already. Her memory, the intimate still beauty you yearned to look upon, that went with it, gone with the first drop of your heart's blood. Be at peace. What is the face of a woman? It will have faded. Beauty is the first of the things that vanish. Lie quiet, then. I have not lost the skill of my fingers. Though the blade is sharp, I wield it quickly. Cold it is, colder than anything in the world but it will ease the fire her warm words left with you. So the second drop takes away bitterness." She paused. "It cannot be called healing. Yet a man can live with it."

"And the third?" Wyck said.

She heard the awe in his voice and looked up at him curiously. Measuring the thinness of his chest and shoulders, her old face hardened. "You have no wound," she said almost silently, something taking her breath.

"He is a boy," I said in his place. "He has never loved."

For the first time she raised her eyes to me. The white length of my hair hung down the sides of my cheeks. Watching how she stared, my hand rose to smooth it. But she was still, her stillness, deep and unbroken as a stone's, spreading through the great room until only the twisting fire fought it, struggling to keep its breath. The sleeves of her gown lay heavily over her wrists, concealing the small tip of the knife. Her voice was low when she spoke.

"Daughters I have had," she whispered, "white as

the pebbles that wash on the shore, daughters black as blood and as many as apples. And sons with them, sons like the foam of the seawaves that raid the coast, sons dark as the seeds of the fruit left rotting in autumn. White and dark are my children." Her hard eyes remained fixed on me. "Yet you are none of them."

I was silent.

"Many I have welcomed to my bed. With the onset of winter, when the sea was clamped with ice and land lay hard as any stone, then they began to think of my hearth with longing. So they came to my door. And though they were webbed or scaled, husbands I made of them. Though they slid or flew, though their breath froze my neck, yet I welcomed them." Her deep eyes shone. "Yet, lord, you are none of them."

My scribe is nodding.

"Which are the daughters?" *I ask him.*

His fingers are blue with the cold. It is almost morning but the guards are still asleep on the benches. I have ordered the doors left open. Through the gaping hole I will watch the sun rising. Invisible, beyond the gray mountains, its feeble light trembles. Nor will it soon rise high enough to warm the souls or even the bones of the men who lie at the hall's end, breathing and tangled in dreams.

"Which?" *I say again to prompt him.*

A dreaming man offers a groan.

The little scribe straightens. He gives me a false and shining smile to prove he is awake. His pages lie scattered about on the floor. He plucks one up, discards it, finds another. Finally, with a kind of shame, he asks, "Lord, would it be on the land, you mean?" *His head is rigid.*

"Yes."

"And the sea?" *He is hoping for light. Surely the cook will come soon, he thinks, and set the dogs barking and the men crawling up backward out of their sleep,*

*stretching, cursing their joints' stiffness and demanding
drink, men swollen-eyed and sick of dreaming, men
little eager for tales.*

"Yes." I remind him.

"There was Ryth," he says slowly, "Sanngion. And
Grieve."

"And with the seablood?"

"Géar."

"And before her?"

"Yllvere, who ruled us, and the Mughain, who ruled
only women."

"And before?"

*He stammers, but no words come out of him. Perhaps
he can hear them, panting and whistling; or buried in
darkness, perhaps he is listening to the whisper of fins.
Like a frightened child's, his eyes have rolled back in
his head.*

"And there were men," the old woman said softly,
"hairy and naked, coming out of the sea." For a moment the great room seemed empty except for the
strangled breath of the fire and the strange scent that
came to my nostrils. Tears ran along the cheeks of the
woman.

Her eyes half closed. "You should be one of them. Yet
it is hard to tell just what you are—you who bear the
third and cruelest wound, that which takes away most,
yet is kindest, for it takes away memory." She lifted her
hands. The sleeve of her gown fell back along the white
length of her arms. "Yet you hold fast to it."

Her eyes were open.

From far off I heard my own voice whispering, "Lady,
I have put on flesh again."

For a little while she was silent. Yet all at once,
though she held her back to it, I saw the firelight dance
in her eyes. "Long we have looked across the world at
one another," she said. "Before the first men came up

on the shore, before the beasts walked there or the iron-shouldered fishes crawled in the waves, across the deep—when not even the first timid stars were there to light it—I saw you watching me. No liegemen had you then or underkings. They were my gift to you. But the sea was between us. So out of myself I made a son to warm me, licking open his eyes so he could look on me. Pale as the dawn he was, as red as the evening, but his face was like nothing but myself. Because you were not in him, I sent him away from me, out into the whirling darkness, far from the world. Then I could see your face again. But because I was still alone, I called him back. So between his coming and going I have lived. So I have grown old. . . . Now you are in my house." She waited. There was no fear in her. "Lord," she said, "I had thought you were too proud."

"It was not pride."

She smiled. "It cannot be you meant it humbly."

"What is done is done," I said. "It is hard to change that."

"Still, for my sake, he will war with you."

"I shall bear it."

The old woman laughed. "Then there is no help for it. It cannot be otherwise than I must bear it also. Yet I would know why you would have it so."

"There was a woman once," I said. "White as the stone she was, dark . . ." I hesitated, watching as she sat above the body of the man. Her strength was fire, the fire that comes out of stone, that cracks its own heart out of gentleness. Her eyes were shining. I said, "I have not forgotten. Lady, I would not forget."

When he saw us, Eachanhagen hurried out from under the trees. "Now we shall ride!" he shouted. It was not yet dawn. A vague light, broken by the count- less faults in the leaves and branches, spread over the grassy yard like rain. Impatient, he splashed through the gloom, bearing a heavy saddle on the ledge of his shoulder, a bit in his hand. But until we had come away from the house, he would not greet us. His eyes wandered in every direction except the one that would have him look at it.

"We shall ride," he shouted again.

He had begun to bridle the stallion and kept his head close to its neck, gazing off through the trees. He moved quickly.

"You have my thanks," Glas Awyddn said.

Eachanhagen stroked the stallion's nuzzle. He did not look up, would not gaze at the pale, emaciated face that, if it were not healed, was at least a face again. "It was cold," he said hoarsely.

"Truly," Glas Awyddn answered him, "it was that."

"Though her fire warmed the air," Eachanhagen whispered, "though the sparks danced and the logs of her trees roared in the hearth..."

Glas Awyddn winced. "Still I could not keep from shivering." But he stopped, for he saw well enough that Eachanhagen knew what it was: to become an emptiness beyond measure, a void that nothing filled, that no fire, however hot, could warm. Indeed, each man knew it, but the boy did not. Rather it seemed to him that the fire had wrapped all about him, had held him blessed, safe in its ease, in its soft, inexhaustible warmth— like a child.

"It was only the smell," Wyck said, "that troubled me." Even in memory his nostrils wrinkled with disgust. He breathed again deeply, to drive it away with the smell of the day.

"She is old," I told him, "and dying."

Wyck looked at me strangely. His jaw hardened. "No," he said. "How shall death have her? It was the smell of the corpses."

One of the stallions whickered. The sealmen were leading the excited horses into the yard. The bridles, studded with silver, gleamed in the murk. The horses pawed at the ground.

"In the corners," Wyck said, "where the fire scarcely reached, in the high rafters, three corpses, hanged as from the gallows..." He rubbed the back of his neck. "...Three heads dangling, vile and rotting, but not asleep. Lord," he said, his voice surprised, "were you not listening? Through the night she spoke with them."

Glas Awyddn cast a glance at me. The wolf's grin that once he had lost pulled again at his lips.

The scribe mutters gravely.

"Which are the dead?" *I ask him.*

"There are many," *he answers.* "How shall a man remember them? Even I cannot, though you have filled me with names."

I sit and wait.

There is only silence. The sun has yet to climb above the gray mountains. He looks around and behind him. He would like to hear a noise, but there is only the sound of his breath.

"The boy not yet come to manhood," *he says at last to keep away silence,* the husband, the..."

"They were ourselves," said Glas Awyddn.

Wyck shook his head. He was only a boy. When they brought up the horses he smiled.

"Where came this horse?" I asked them. I did not add, Where should such men find him, a horse like winter and white snow, a horse without blemish or peer, walking easily out of the morning? He came slowly, treading the soft green turf, his eight legs moving regally, his matched gait stately as mourners shouldering a bier. He dropped his broad forehead, meeting my own.

"Where?" I repeated.

"You shall judge that yourself," a man at my side said thickly. He was afraid to look at the stallion and did not move his head.

Yet another man whispered, "Lord, he came from the wood."

The sealmen were quiet. They stared back toward the trees, toward the deep wood through which they had passed in the evening, through whch they must go again, though soon the sun would fill it. A light breeze wafted into the yard, bearing the sweet scent of leaves. Eager they were to be going, yet the gladness had gone from them, and they shivered. But whatever the sealmen thought, Wyck beamed.

He said in wonder, "Never have I seen such a horse."

"Nor will you ever see the like of him," Eachanhagen answered, his face thoughtful and still when he turned to me. "Yet he has come to you," he said. "For surely there is not one among all of us, only yourself, who would ride him."

Even then Wyck would have reached for his mane. "Just for a moment," he pleaded. I met his eyes.

"Indeed, lord," he said quietly, "he is yours." He turned aside quickly, finding his own. The dust from the prancing horses hid his face. He jerked at the reins.

Glas Awyddn took hold of the mount I had ridden. One by one, the sealmen climbed onto the backs of their horses until no man was standing. They lifted their necks and swung their wide shoulders. Impatient, a man called out. But though the horses stamped, not one sprang forward.

Eachanhagen's brows came together meditatively. "The horses know him," he said, "if men do not. Swift and tireless these horses are, and great-hearted as kings.

More sense they have than men. They will not walk ahead of him."

I pulled myself up. Beneath my legs I felt the great strength of the stallion, the width of his hard, thickened spine, the muscles rippling effortlessly under his flesh. "If he leads," I said, "they must follow him."

Eachanhagen smiled. "Even such a horse," he said, "has a master."

I lifted my arm and went, with the horses trotting behind me, under the trees. If a woman stood by the door, I did not look back. So a man does not look twice at a stone. I did not grieve. It is so simple a truth that any child knows it. However masked and hidden, the wide earth is everywhere the same. It cannot be otherwise. Whatever a man passes waits ahead of him. Else which of her sons would be bold enough to poke his nose out of doors?

By the time we were well under the branches the breeze had softened, bringing a mist. Not the great mist such as rolls in for weeks together upon the coast at Brehnum-Sawle. This did not come by force. Rather it crept between roots and slunk around hooves. Here and there, thickened, it cloistered in hollows, pale as the froth in discarded caldrons. A chill came with it.

Eachanhagen, his sharp breath fogged, rode with his fur cap pulled down over his ears. He had hidden the fingers of one hand under his arm. But for myself I was not discontented. In truth, I found a strange comfort in the mists' gentle drifting, gentler than the coming of the tides, sweeping as softly into the morning as the first cool rains in autumn.

Some miles from the house the land sloped down. The ground turned soggy and wet. Emboldened, the mist climbed from the horses' knees to their withers; it dripped in their hair. The shapes of the trees grew dim, and their branches came at me suddenly out of the air. I picked my way carefully so that the horses could follow. A wind sprang up, but it was sullen and wet and blew nothing away. Through the dampness I heard the men cursing. They had their right. We were longer leaving the wood than going into it. More often I gave the great horse his head. He took me gladly then, his hoofbeats quickening; as though he judged my height, I was less troubled by the switch of branches and the tearing of brambles against my legs. No longer bending double, the riders edged up closer. The great horse stepped lightly in front of them. Nevertheless, it was a long slow business. Though we had little to look at, the day was wearing. The mist grew raw. On the edges of its whiteness there were shadows.

"They are but trees we pass," said a flat voice from back in the line.

"This is still her wood."

A man snorted. "And they are still trees."

"No." It was Eachanhagen then, his tired voice rumbling deep in his chest. "They are taller and older. Much taller and a great deal older, I think, and less likely to stay where she put them."

A man laughed recklessly.

I looked behind, but there was only the cloud of mist, the jingle of bridles. I rubbed my smarting eyes and listened. There was a noise like wind ruffling leaves. A gentle wind or very far off. They are not small trees certainly, I thought. For, if I saw nothing, I felt their hugeness. The horses lumbered blind beneath their shadows. Somewhere, in the highest branches, an evening lark sang. The same man coughed.

"I would ride the plain again," he said.

"He must find what he seeks here."

"I pray he finds it quickly then," the man grumbled. He said little else and yet the words stung me. I knew what was fitting and what was not. Truly, we had come a long way and gone nowhere. Nonetheless, I needed no man's groaning.

The ears of my stallion were bent in the damp. Watching them, I gave vent to my anger. "See that it is my own business that takes you," I scolded. The stallion neighed blissfully and went on as before.

If there were ground under us, it went upward.

When I cared to look, I saw nothing. But the trees were there, unseen and unquiet. Their strange leaves were tossing. The stallion lifted his head. A frost seemed to creep through his shoulders. I plucked at his mane.

As I straightened, he veered all at once. His long neck lunged forward. His hooves barely struck at the stones. I heard the oaths of the sealmen as they straggled behind. Bolted awake, they drove their heels into the flanks of the horses. Fearful, they hurled themselves upward. Yet as suddenly the way had grown clear. Mists that had clung uncoiled their fingers. Mists that had blotted out hills slunk down around stones. Then it was, though the air itself was darkening, I first saw the trees, trees ageless and black, trees towering over the gray earth as only the One Tree rose above Morrigan.

We had climbed a steep bank. To the west, beyond the ridge, the wood dropped away to the plain. Already fallen, the sun gave no light to it. Yet so great was their height that the topmost branches yet watched it and kindled with flame. I rode looking up.

The stallion jerked his head nervously.

Heedless, I was urging him onward. At the raw edge a stone loosened and fell. In that moment I saw the pit under me.

Slipping down from their mounts, the sealmen stood about staring, their faces turned grave and quiet in the hush of the evening. It was Wyck who broke it. Pointing

out with a hand that trembled, he touched ever so
gently the flank of my stallion, brushing a clod of earth
from his hair.

"Lord?" he said softly.

"I have eyes of my own to watch with," I said.

The bank was pulled wide, wrenched open like jaws.
Tendrils were snarled at its brink. Farther down the
carnage of old twisted roots poked out through the
walls, the nest of wood sundered and split as though
cracked and torn upward when the thing that long had
stood there had awakened and climbed from the earth.

"There are black trees over us," Eachanhagen said.

The sealmen drew back and looked at the stallion. As
they watched him, his great chest heaved deeply and
they saw the pale shine of his throat and the width of
his shoulders. The eight thick legs under him stood
monstrous in the dusk. Forcing themselves to believe,
the sealmen kept their eyes open. But the darkness
muffled their voices. I did not need to hear.

"Surely," I told them, "there was one that was white."

"A horse?"

"A ship," I repeat. "It is the breaking waves that are
called the horses of the sealmen, but the ninth is Gwen
Gildrun. It was myself long ago who planted it, in the
wood above Morrigan. But it was a ship before and
after, and a horse only when I had need of it."

The boy looks at his hands. He came from the
kitchen because a boy must come when a king calls him
though the grown men laugh and the women, back by
the ovens, shake their old heads. He would prefer, I
know, the work in the stables or in the high barn,
where from the windows, facing the north and east, he
can watch my grim soldiers riding out to the wars. But
it takes half a morning for the thralls to find him there,
and the kitchen is closer to hand.

He has but lately come and his fingers are coated with grease. He rubs their sides in his hair to clean them. Because I will not long suffer his silence, at last he looks up.

He answers me quietly. "The *filidh* say they are sheep. That ninth is a ram." His voice is low.

Out in the dawn there are crows. I can hear them flocking down from the roofpeaks. They prance on the cobbles, their black feet tapping lightly like blind men with sticks. Before the last bright star faded, they were awake, seeking the vermin that nest in the thatch. But not even their hunger can keep them. Before the cook rises or the first soldier, muttering, reaches out for his boots, the crows will have gone. The blue morning beckons them. Like boys and old kings, they can make do without sleep.

I rest my long arms on the chair. "That is not different. Whether horses or sheep, they must come as I call them. If you would have listened, you would have heard. They were the Redd Man's once. But now they are mine again."

His dark eyes look out from under their shadows. "Must a thing be what a man calls it?"

I see the trap. "*Things* must be."

"And men?"

I press my great hands against his smooth shoulders. Under the narrow flesh the bone is as thin as a crow's. Soon enough it will thicken. Already in his eyes there is too much cleverness. I think, *I have had my peace. Even a king cannot keep the seed in the ground or a god, the new sun from pulling free of earth*. And yet I would hold him. I say, "There was a woman once."

"A goddess?" he asks dutifully.

"Yes." My voice breaks. "It was Anu. . . . In the dark of one evening I rode through her wood. A company of men I had with me, trotting behind. . . ."

He is not listening.

The soldiers have come in at the door, taking his sight. Not a man of them is mighty or tall, but their legs are well girded and their broad backs heavy with iron. Beyond the wall of the mountain the sun has already lifted its head. The yellow light burns on the metal. The boy stops his breath.

"Llugh."

I turned, but it was only a sealman muttering, jolted awake in his saddle, the sun in his face.

Silently, during the night, we had come down through the trees, the sealmen no more awake than their horses, passing quietly westward down the slopes of the hills. The trees had grown smaller, more like the trees men knew, chestnut and maple and oak. They stood farther back—until now and then in the ragged holes between branches there had been stars, winking and bright in the evening. But gradually the darkness behind them had faded. Then at last we had come to the edge of a stream. Upon its smooth surface I had caught the first glint of dawn. There had been deep prints of hooves at the ford, there before us and gone. He has found horses, I thought. I had touched the cold flank of my stallion. He had lengthened his stride. So we had passed quickly over the water and come out on the far side from under the eaves of the wood and onto the green plain, turned gold in the morning.

My stallion snorted and sniffed at the air.

"He has scented an animal," Eachanhagen said. But I knew he had not.

My eyes went back to the road. It came out of the north, cutting beneath the shoulder of a hill, then wound away southward and eastward. It skirted the edge of the wood, which marched along beside it, just out of reach. Gleams of sunlight struck the stones, turning the road tawny and brown, the colors of autumn. I gazed over it thoughtfully. At the farthest edge of sight there was a mountain. Vague and colorless, it floated on the world's rim as though neither land nor sea were certain where it stood or which would claim it.

"Should a man find this road," I said, "would he come at last among the Penandrun?"

"Lord, it is traveled," Eachanhagen said. "There would be men to find him now."

"And if he would not be found?"

"Lord, it is a road. It goes where it goes. A man would follow it."

Glas Awyddn stroked his raven beard and laughed. "What way is there left to you, my king, but into trouble? I never heard a man went looking for a war and never found it."

"Men may do as they please," I said impatiently. Giving a nudge to the stallion, I sent him out along the stones.

The great road widened as we went, as the slightest stream widens, until as it spread it seemed an army might have moved along it, rank by rank. Indeed, the plates of stone were worn with use, and some were cracked. In places, where after rains the mud had seeped down from the banks, there were ruts and holes. Here once, by the look of them, enormous wagons must have mired before the soldiers, swearing at their teams, had pushed the thick wheels out and on again. Elsewhere the grass itself, like an arm of the tide, had washed across it. But whether mud or grass had covered it, there were stones beneath. Well set and solid, laid with a careful eye, they remained the lasting proof that men had made the road and that, however the sea had changed them, those men were landsmen once. Hurt by the harsh, incisive brightness of the stones, my tired eyes left them and blinked.

Eachanhagen rode just behind me. I did not need to look at him.

"As easily I might have looked north," I said. "Myself, I chose to ride southward, to the mountain and the old ones' court."

I heard his silence.

"Not a man of us came unknowing his fate," he said at last. "If you go to the Penandrun, we must follow you. If you linger there, in the sea-girt hall, trading tales with men grown too old and stretched for death, what shall we do but sit with you and listen? How are you different? Soon enough you will long to see the North again, to climb beyond the place where this road is broken and walk on the shore." He sighed. "Even the tide goes back and forth. How then shall the heart of a king keep from turning?"

"It would depend," I said, "on what he was lord of."

His stallion lurched forward. "You are the Promised One!" he cried.

"Llugh," a man whispered from back in the line. As though the word were an echo it rose from the plain, gathered a strength from the trampling of horses and a will from their breath. "Llugh," the host whispered. "Llugh."

Glas Awyddn laughed.

Below me to the left the road ran down into a hollow. Bent sharply eastward, beyond the tongue of the wood, it seemed to vanish. Trees and wild bracken encroached on the stones. Away to the south the road swept back again, but close at hand the signs of stonework faded under deepening shadows. The sealmen knew this place. Giving no thought to it, they rode contentedly, talking among themselves. Wyck rode in the midst of the troop, his face open, his mount trotting easily. At the front I was alone with Glas Awyddn.

A smoky light lit up the branches. One or two of the trees were red, with the sun's death or with autumn.

"He has horses now," I said, "and has gone ahead of us."

"The three of them?"

"They are as we are. Bound as we are bound."

"Even the boy?"

I looked at him gloomily. "He—alone of all the earth—is free of me. That was my right, though never before have I used it. Yet when the battle comes, perhaps at the end of it, when hope is least, he will serve me. I cannot tell. It was fate that trapped me into pitying. Fate must see what comes of it. How shall I weigh the chance? Though once again I have shouldered my memory, one mystery I have kept, even from myself."

I was silent after that. But Glas Awyddn went rushing on, leaping swiftly from what was to what might be, holding his balance by fierceness, as a man crosses a torrent, stone by stone.

"But for Wyck," he said, "you know the end."

"Yes."

"And the Penandrun?"

"They are the first of singers. As it is their song, they know its telling."

His eyes watched me, eyes that could pierce a man though they were in my service. "Then they will see the fault," he said.

"See and then forget it too. Too often they have sung the tale. Too well they know it. For in every deed they see the broad tale stretching out, all that was its cause and all as well that springs up after, until there is nothing that is itself, that does not bear the shape of all the rest. How then does it matter if it is Llugh, in fact, who comes to them? From their great halls, looking out, they shall see a bold man riding down the sea's bright plain. They are not gulled or cheated. A man comes riding. They know the rest. At whatever point I enter, the tale runs on from it."

His hand was still in his beard. He said, "Llugh rides before us. He will be first in the halls."

"Which is first?" I asked.

"Lord?"

"Was it darkness or light?"

His face grew long and he looked with greater interest at his knees. "Lord," he said sullenly, "I am only a man."

I smiled. "Then be at peace," I said, "for it is not for you to manage it."

There was silence again, except for the clop of hooves and the horses' breathing, and after a little while— somewhere out ahead, beyond where the road turned and was hidden—a whisper. The sky was still light, but the light trembled and grew thin. The horses were beginning to shake their heads. I listened. Halfway along the curve of the road, where it sank farther down into the hollow and the trees that crowded its eastern edge pulled back like a hedge, there was a barley field. Unswerving, the road ran straight through it. The seed had not been sown to either side but had grown up between the stones, ignoring them, as though the great old road were an inconvenience that would pass. At the corner of the field a tall old man, his wide shoulders covered by a coat, was cutting the barley. The last slanting sunlight dappled his back. As he mowed, the blade rang out softly.

"Reaper," I called out to him, "have you seen a man riding ahead of us?"

Toward the end of each stroke the old man leaned forward. He did not look up. "I have been mowing since daybreak, lord," he grumbled. "Still the work is not finished. What time do I have to look at the road?"

"It is but a little field."

The barley fell in neat rows to his left, one after another unceasingly. "Truly," he said, "it is no greater than that. Yet it is great enough. For whatever I cut keeps on growing. Still, I mean to finish. This is my field. I plowed it when it was only salt, and when it grew I watched over it." He groaned faintly. "That was not the work of a moment. Nor is this. So, lord, by your leave, I will wish good day to you."

My smile only deepened. The last light faded red from the blade of the scythe. It was dark then. The sealmen, who could no longer see one another, stumbled up from behind, leading their horses. They kept their feet on the stones, inching forward. Eachanhagen groped with his hands. "Lord," he called out. Several times he had shouted.

"I am here," I said, "but come no farther. There is a field in front of me but it would be a gristly thing to come into it. Tie your horses where they are and do not let them feed in the stubble."

"Lord," Eachanhagen said crossly, "this will not be the first time we have been here." I had touched his pride. "What is a field?" he said. "Along the road there are many."

"This," I said, "has a man in it."

"So there was when we rode out, an old reaper in a long red coat taking the barley. What do I care of that?" Though he knew the rest heard him, he had made his voice loud. "There have always been reapers," he added.

"Indeed," I said, "but then I have not always been with you."

He was a brave man, but he had only the darkness to look at. Though he had been coming forward, he took a step back.

* * *

They did not strain their eyes when the late moon rose, peering down at the plain. For each man there was only breath and snoring. Even the horses, huddled together, were asleep. Hunched, sunk down on a stone, I had begun my watch. The field was shining. The sky above it, though it had never yielded its blackness, shone with a steady, unbroken light. I sat and waited.

"It is getting late," the reaper said.

I looked around and saw him standing alone in the silver stubble. He looked old, older than I remembered him. Wearily, he lifted his coat. Out of an inside pocket he extracted a grease jar and from another a hone. When the coat was open, I saw the rest of his arms.

"He will come."

"He but lately walked," the reaper said. "Though already he thinks himself grand, his mother's lap still seems wide to him. In the quiet, when night comes and the mists that climb the Mound take shape against him, he hides himself in her hair."

"Glas Awyddn has seen him," I said. "He has given him armor."

The reaper made no answer.

My voice grew stern. "Yourself," I said, "have carried him across the river."

He had set the jar down and the hone with it. "I do not deny it, lord," he said. "Here I carried him. And never have I felt such lightness for he was as nothing in my arms." Reaching out, he took the hone. When it had dripped, he rolled it over the sand. "But you," he groaned, "were a torment in my knees and on my back a bitterness."

His eyes narrowed and he began to sharpen the scythe. "But the men I bore here were never living men—only men who were or those who yet would be." He shook his head. "On land, at least, he is a boy. Nine years will she keep him with her on the Mound. Twice nine again must follow before at Tywy he comes to you."

"There is a man riding," I said.

And though before there had been nothing but a field and the moon gently gilding the stubble, of a sudden a man was riding, handsome and tall, on a horse pale as dawn. He came, passing out of the field's emptiness and into the light, as day comes, out of itself, not from shadows. I saw his brow then, white as a stone against darkness, unwrinkled as stone—for as yet no grief had come to him, his new life unsung and untroubled. He came to the top of the field where the barley was cut. There he let the stallion drop his pale head to graze on the stubble.

"Good evening, little one," I said to him.

He smiled, his deep eyes searching over the field. When he found where I was, he went on smiling. "As well my greeting, lord, though I doubt that I am less than you."

Indeed he was taller than any man had been except myself. But I said, "Who is there to judge between us here? Let it be. What comes, comes soon enough. At Tywy we will settle it and not before. Now I am only glad to look at you." Still, I saw how, smiling, he watched me, taking the measure of my legs and shoulders.

"This is my realm," he said.

I laughed. "Child, I got you born in it."

The lips like my own pulled back. "I was not certain, lord, that you would say it." It seemed that for a moment I saw a flash of redness on his cheeks. But then it was autumn and he was but partway in this place, and there were blazing oaks in back of him. He said, "On land you will not claim me."

"There she will have you to herself."

"Lord," he answered simply, "she never knew a man but once. She never had a woman's life but that one day she took you to the Mound."

"It was her choosing."

He went on smiling. "She never looked for any other. But because of it she will fill all the days that now must come with memory—your shape, your words . . . your hand upon her in the dark." For a moment silence crept into his mouth.

"Lord," he said slowly, "though now I am too young to know the grief of that, in time I must. And when that sorrow comes, it will be always with me, a pain that never sleeps or lets me rest. The god knows I will hate you then."

I watched him quietly. "Child, I know it." But I saw as well that it was only a tale to him and laughed. He looked relieved.

And yet his fingers closed about his reins. "I am going south to the halls," he said. It was nothing idle. The words were judged.

"In time," I said, "when it is fitting and the turning comes to it."

"I am here," he answered. "By whatever cause, even your own. I have a horse and men to go with me."

In the deep field, farther off, I saw the shapes that sometimes were Glas Awyddn and sometimes Wyck. And sometimes not. My long jaw set a little. "It is their everlasting deaths to go with you," I said, "now, before their time. Your choice, and the price for it, to take them."

He smiled but the smile was grander then. "How shall you strike at me?" he said. The great smile deepened. "This realm is mine. And they are mine who come with me. I mean no insult to your strength. Yet, lord, how shall you raise the least hand here when even the flesh you are clothed in is my own?"

"I will not."

"Lord?"

"Child, this is not your field, or mine." I turned my neck and with the turning he saw the old one standing out ahead of me. His hands were warty from his trades, his coat too big so it could hold his arms. The moon rose higher. Even then its cold light was lost in the wool of his hair, slid down the sides of his huge shoulders. But on the long curve of the scythe it was burning.

"I have my work," the reaper said.

The boy's smile was frozen. "I do not stand in the way of it," he said softly. But he contrived to look some other way. A breath of air, imperceptible to his flesh, reached out for the barley. The small heads murmured. He would not listen. But something in the shape and color of the night made him aware of what his eyes would see, what his ears would hear, if he would make use of them. He plucked at the reins, then took hold of them deliberately, pulling the head of his great horse away from the stubble. There was something dripping from the stallion's mouth. Between his jaws a thing cracked.

He said, "I have no part in this."

"When I gave you life, you took it gladly."

He did not move. The night was cold and, though his hands were colder, I saw how he steadied them. I saw as well how his eyes looked out from under their shadows. In the south, low and black on the horizon, under the cold stars, in the halls of the Penandrun there were men and armies, waiting.

"Why have you brought me here?" he said.

"Once, child, before I murder you, to see your face."

The field, the center of the field where the barley and the sea road met, was empty. In the hush toward dawn, the sealmen stirred. Beneath their labored breath, in the fields and halls, in the sweeping seas and windy beaches at the ends of sleep, they heard thinly, if at all, the echo of hooves retreating, going north along the road. Though if they heard, they did not think to follow. In some other place they were lords and kings. But here they were soldiers, and soldiers follow what is nearest them. They slept again.

Because I did not sleep, I had been walking on the margins of the road, walking slowly, stopping now and then to stir with my foot whatever I could find—a piece of straw rope, a broken drag dropped from the back of a brewer's wagon and abandoned on the stone. The dew, if it can be called dew undersea, was heavy. My hair was wet. I touched it, fingering its strangeness, knowing it was not my own. I was alone—for the first time since I had seen Glas Awyddn swimming in the sea.

Off in the chilly wood a bird was squealing.

"Has he gone?"

I spun around. Wyck was standing in the road. Wrapped in what was left of my cloak, he grinned.

"I heard you talking—I was asleep and it woke me." He yawned and pulled the cloak more tightly around his neck.

"You choose your time ill," I said harshly. "You were better off sleeping."

He shrugged. "It was better I was Glas Awyddn's dog boy, but you have seen to it that I am not."

He walked beside me. A breeze, passing through the wood, blew the first dried leaves across our path. In the south, before the lesser darkness, the nine peaks began to shape themselves against the sky.

"Lord," he said, "I was content. I did not need to see my life stretched out. Like any man, I would have had my strength grow less and less."

"Why do you not sleep?"

His head came up. "Why, lord, have you taken death from me?"

"Have you finished?"

"If you will answer that." He paused, his dark eyes watching.

I touched his hair, a boy's fine hair that year by year would never coarsen. But even then my eyes strayed past him, following the road's faint ribbon north between the hills. No figure turned.

"He would not take the gift," I said.

The peaks grew brighter as day came. In time, drawing up behind, the sealmen brought our horses.

A day more and in the distance there were wagons—small, odd wagons of uncertain cargo, pressing purposefully toward the south. From the back of my stallion I counted twenty and twenty more and could have kept on counting but for the dust raised by wheels and the sudden knots where some by mischance halted and the line backed up. There were men on horses and men trotting along beside the jolting wagons, men with flocks and men with herds, men striding alone in the midst of their beasts and darting with them when they turned. But all went southward, returning to the winter pasturage at summer's end.

Wyck gazed silently across the endless stream, as a child gazes at a river and wonders at its source.

"Where do their numbers come?" he said at last.

"From the North."

"No," he said. "I did not mean that." I saw him square his shoulders and take his grip more firmly on the reins. "In this place," he said quietly, "how are there more of them?"

So any child must ask the one great question whose answer he has already guessed.

"Being what they are," he said, "what this place is."

"Being men."

"And stallions, bulls, and rams."

I did not answer. My eyes went back along the road.

"How do they increase?" he said again, unashamed at last to show his impatience.

I could hear their voices now, the noise and jostling, the braying and bleating, the oaths of men.

Glas Awyddn laughed. Still, his eyes held little mirth. "The Redd Man keeps at his work," he said.

We passed the stragglers first, men in indifferent, neglected dress, advancing sideways, their necks craned back, not intent on us but on the land behind, the all-consuming brightness of the autumn sky, the fields they had left. Their nostrils flared, trying to keep the last scent of the grass.

"Is there still some summer in the North?" a man asked sulkily. He had only felt my horse beside him and did not look up. As though he hardly noticed that he spoke aloud, he said, "I warned them we had gone too soon. There were yet fish in the pools. There were stalks we had not gathered. Nor was the wind so harsh. I would have borne it." His little restless eyes fixed on nothing I could see, he gave a drawn-out sigh. I did not answer it. There is no use in speaking to the newly dead. Their heads are filled only with memory.

Though dead as well, the sheep moved skittishly. Bounding among their brothers, leaping on their backs, they went on breathing the damp close odors of wool and hide, indifferently. So they had always moved, in vast, distrustful flocks, ignorant of all misfortunes but their own. Death little changed that. But the herdsmen, accustomed to keeping watch, turned their quick, harsh eyes upon us. Not a man spoke to me. Still, they dipped their heads. I felt the name they whispered, changed to eagerness. Smiles came out of their faces.

"Come along, Dinas. Come along, Vawr. Come along, you black-faced devils," they shouted. "In the Penandrun's

halls there are barns to shut you in, warm cribs and hay
to keep your bellies warm when the hail comes biting."

The road was better then, built with smooth gray
stones and more often tended. Even the sprawling
grass had been swept back on the banks, and the
larches that had grown too close cut down to keep their
spreading fingers from poking off the caps of the wagoners. The banks were steep, for here, as well, in wet
weather the mud moved down from the fields and had
to be flung up on either side. The sun, in the middle of
its height, threw a brightness without warmth at the
sweating horses. Men shouted out to them across their
rumps. Rocking back and forth on the stones, the
wagons thundered.

As our line passed them the sharp faces of the
wagoners turned toward me. Their eyes, that were
used to wonders, that had been left dull and blank with
death and then reborn, those same eyes burned. They
were not soldiers. They would not fight or meet again
the mostrous dread. Llugh would not marshal them nor
make corpses of them twice; yet they were his folk and
knew the promise. Like any soldier, they stood to gain
the land. Their eyelids flickered; their tongues came
out indecently.

A man without a cap to hide his ragged hair stared up
at me from his wagon. He had set his hand before his
lips, afraid to speak.

"What do you wish?" I said.

"Shall we be whole again?" he stammered, but I saw
that it was only part of what he meant.

"You have legs and arms."

He shook his head and the rest of him shook with it.
He blinked with fear and cunning. Like a worn old
cloth his mouth split wide. "Lord," he grinned, "are
there women still?"

I stopped to wait for Eachanhagen to catch up with

me. He came slowly, for from every wagon questions came at him: Was I in truth the Promised One? If I were meant to come in glory, why was it the small one wore my cloak? Why was it torn? When would I gather the armies? If not by winter, would it be by spring? When could they expect to see their towns again, their farms at Brehnum-Sawle, at Tyre, the marsh at Mhor? Did sweet william grow in gardens still? Would I remember that, but lately come? Did housewives yet dry hops against the chimneys? Were vines still planted deep? Did it rain on the Eve of Teimhne last? Or was it snow as always? Would all, for certain, come with me when I went to Tywy?

He answered what he could, though that was little, and shouted that surely I would make plain as much as I wanted when we made the halls, that for himself he was content with that and they should ask no more.

"They fill the road," I said to him when his stallion had drawn abreast of mine.

"They are many. But year by year there are more."

"There were few," I said, "by the river when we crossed."

Eachanhagen stiffened his back. "Only kings and armed men cross there. For that is the grandest place. But there are a thousand streams. Truly, not a trickle runs seaward but somewhere along it a redd man is waiting. Men find them, men like any other but unlike soldiers, not looking for death but only running down to fetch rushes or, their minds elsewhere, driving the red oxen to drink in the shallows. It does not matter, so long as there is water to cross. You would not know this. The highborn never do. Those with their forged swords and armor, who courted death, give little thought to men who blunder into it, whom death takes just as surely but unaware."

"Their lords are no less dead."

His brown cheeks reddened. "It is not the same."

"Yourself, you were a soldier."

"Was," he said. "Am," he went on in a disgusted voice; "will ever be." He paused. "Yet once I was a diker, as low a man as these men are. Ten years I drained the fens, awash in slop, making fields with a wooden shovel for them who were lords and owned marshes but wanted land. I was but two years a soldier. War came and they took my shovel and put a spear in its place. So I made death instead."

"And came, when death took you, by the grandest way into *Tir fo Thuinn*. And were put ahead of other men."

"So I might fight again."

"Would you change it?"

He was not old. There was not so much as a single gray hair on his head. He had a sword in his belt and in his left hand a lance with three sharp points. Along beside him the wagons pitched and rolled. The faces of the wagoners, like burning masks, looked out at us with fear and envy. He did not turn his head.

He said, "I know the work." A deep, heartbroken pride showed in his face. Ahead, in the shadow of the banks, an old man with a wooden shovel was clearing black mud from the stone.

Farther on there were other bands of wagons but the same smell of men and the turf smell of horses on the thick evening air. There were horsemen as well, gathered in from the plain, riding in through the heather and the waist-deep weed. The tireless green horses climbed over the embankments with care. The long shadows of lances grew like a brown thicket at my left hand. No man cried out. Yet one by one their chiefs rode up the line to look at me. Perhaps Eachanhagen spoke to them. I heard only the quick hoofbeats trotting back.

The sound washed soft then hard, then soft then hard again, like waves against stone. So, alone on my great ship, I had heard the gray sea lapping the hull. The waves had seemed like hoofbeats then. It made no difference. The waves were armies, the horsemen fierce as any cursing sea. And should I walk upon the land, even the boulders there, I knew, would take new life and follow me. Had not the gaunt old stones risen up behind Ar Elon when I had his shape? I had not called them. No more did I call these men.

In darkness, hours I never counted passed. The moon was late; the stars, their dim lights shifted by the upper sea, were unreliable. The sea road rolled away beneath. I no longer listened, not even to the wind, though now it blew with a keener edge. I let my mind drift into darkness, into the soundless holes that worm through sleep, and for a space, between midnight and morning, remembered nothing. So even the least wave cast at heaven hangs for a moment at its height. However cursed, some strength, however fleeting, holds its fall.

I drew an icy breath. It was nearly dawn.

Gray streaks showed for a moment in the east, then with a strange deep quiet the endless rushing cloud poured over us. A hail of grass and tiny broken twigs blew in front of the horses. The rain came after, headlong, pounding the stones. There was no riding into it. Wiping a stream of water from my eyes, I gazed at the size of the army straggling at my back. The long lines of mail-clad men checked their steeds and sent them leaping away from the swollen torrents that gorged on the hills. I sent my own horse up, climbing the fissured and crumbling walls.

A roaring confusion rose and buried what was left of the line. The harnessed horses screamed. At once the road was crammed with wagoners, swimming, scrambling, when they could reach them, to the tops of the wains. Boxes sprang from their stays. Barrels raced off in the current, knocking into the horses. Rolling and tumbling savagely, they piled up like a dam where the road angled sharply until, in a rush, they broke again in one thick mass, like a piece of the bank itself, sliding away out of sight.

A moment passed.

The wind blew wickedly but the rain no longer beat down with any force. A ray of chilly light cut through the cloud. The road, where the tide was draining, seemed suddenly shabby and cold. The horses walked about shivering. On the banks, above the high-water marks, the enterprising sheep stood out with startling clarity. The sky grew paler. Already I could see a few men climbing down, wading out through the mud. Squeezing their caps, they had begun to think how to upend a wagon that had been deposited on its back.

With astonishing speed the soldiers picked up their lances. Once more they slung their painted shields across their shoulders. Soon one or two rode forward. I was quiet watching them. I could hear the air again, moving in the grass. The herdsmen walked slowly down the southward slope. The horsemen gathered, talking among themselves or mending their gear, leaving the wagoners to salvage what they could. There were no hard glances. In the years undersea they had grown used to floods. By midmorning they had made a great pile of sodden hay and barrels, boxes, bound flax and coopered tubs, of jars and bladders and sacks, all that had spilled and floated or had not been too deeply buried and could be dug out and left to dry.

Eachanhagen hesitated. He smiled to himself then took a few steps closer to where I stood, dismounted, staring out at the road.

"Lord, it is time we went," he said.

Silhouetted against the chalky light, I saw the lines of horsemen winding toward us up the brow of the hill. Wyck was with them, near the front, his nose and his chin thrust out proudly. A fur cap he had got hold of somewhere was pulled down snug on his head. For the last time I saw him grinning. He looked as though he had just been in a fight and won. I supposed it was the sea he had fought with.

"And the wagoners?"

"They will take what they can with the wagons left. What they cannot will be come back for."

I grunted, as if unconvinced. "And the drowned men?" I said.

He laughed. It was a good laugh. Truly, though I would have his head on the stones of Tywy, the first wave in, for he was Llugh's and served him, yet I sometimes thought that I would sooner lose myself the service of all the faithless devils with me on the land than never hear the sound of it. He took up the reins of his stallion lightly and found its back. He smiled, his forehead wrinkling.

"They will dig themselves out." He was about to turn, then added, "And those who will not, the next wave will wash free or else the dikers will." He paused, looking down at his own thick arms. "I told you I was one myself. We'll not let them sleep."

I walked on a few paces.

"It will be a bitter war," I said.

For a moment he watched me strangely, then he laughed. "How is it, lord," he asked, "that they will slaughter us?"

Over the days the nine small towers had grown ever larger in the south. By now they took a quarter of the sky, huge as the new dark moon, each looming up so tall it seemed it made its own black night on the climbing hills that rose before us. Along the road there were stands of birch and a few stiff vines. The wood that long had followed us had trailed off to the east, leaving the black hills open. In the fields the grass was thin. I felt the soldiers watching me. I pushed them on. In the evening we came upon houses. Low against the ground, their roofs staved in, they had been abandoned when the wells turned brackish with the rains. The ground still smelled of flood. The men were grumbling. I did not let them rest. The miles went by.

Now some of the hills were walled at their summits but the sentries had been called in; the platforms were empty, the stables cleared. The road bent around beneath their shadows.

Glas Awyddn gazed ahead. The clouds had parted and, though the sky was darkening, the air was clear. "There is something shining underneath the peaks," he said. He rose up in his stirrups. "I have seen it twice between the hills, though the darkness of the towers sometimes blots it out."

"It is the lake that circles about their halls," Eachanhagen said. "Beyond these hills the road lies straight. By morning you will see it plainly."

"And the ships," a soldier close by him said.

Eachanhagen nodded. "And the ships that wait to take us to the land."

Wyck woke after sunrise. Sunk down in his saddle, he had slept for several hours as the last stars faded. His eyes were red. After he woke he sat a long time rocking gently as the stallion, close packed with the other horses, ambled across the long causeway that connected the shore of the lake with the ramparts—still a mile off—of the nine-towered mountain. His thick shoulders rose and fell. He did not look at the ships or the mountain. While the road had run down swiftly on the other side of the hills, turning a wide curve by the harbor, stretching away south again past pens and building yards, he had been dreaming. A cold goose-flesh stood up on his arms. The soldiers nearest him nudged one another and grinned.

At the end of the causeway the nine stone towers rose without preface from the lake. The old stonework glittered, gleaming with a brilliance reflected from the lake. Ancient and tall those towers were: a mountain built on water, the blue rock dragged up from the deepest ocean and set on piles, spread across ledges and islands, a city and a mountain threaded with channels and spanned with bridges, arched and high themselves as hills. Men who knew of it said that in the oldest days the seal-lords who built here built as the god built the world's fastness, with the same sureness, with thought and not with hands. As they neared, the eyes of the sealmen sparkled.

"In all the world there are no halls like these," a sealman said to Wyck. He winked with silent laughter at the boy's long face. Wyck stared at the water gloomily, laced and unlaced his brooding fingers on the reins.

"You smile," Wyck said, "but before many days the winter comes."

The line of the sealman's mouth stretched wide with laughter. "We have the sun," he cried. "How shall it be winter when Llugh dwells with us?" His deep voice boomed, the sound of it carrying across the lake with a strength and joy that reached the farthest walls and echoed back.

Along the line the sealmen looked in each other's eyes. The tales at last were true. Even the shame of dying at a stranger's hands, the hideous quiver in the flesh when the bones were parted, the spray of blood and pain, now seemed as nothing. It was the trade of soldiering. What else could be expected when a man took arms? But all would be paid for now. The faces of the sealmen, looking up, listening with wonder, were lit with the same conviction and delight.

The glimmering colors of the harbor danced on the stone. In the first of the towers, high up where the gulls were soaring, a window was open. A shadow moved against the light, passed, and then, distracted, came back again.

The head of a very ancient man thrust itself outside the casement. The light made him blink. The ridges of his forehead were shrouded with dismal patches of hair. Blown in the wind, they lent a kind of uncertainty and shapelessness to the skull. The sealmen found it hard to remember what they saw.

"Grandfather!" a sealman shouted. "Have you not seen? It is Llugh who rides with us!"

The old man straightened. Looking nowhere in particular, he uttered a word. But what it was there was no telling.

The flank of Wyck's stallion brushed against mine. I saw the look of desolation in his face.

"What do you fear so much?" I said quietly.

"In the dark," he whispered, "coming down from the hills . . ." He stopped.

"Child?"

"I dreamed." His eyes went suddenly to my face. "There is another hall," he said, his voice just a whisper above the footfall of horses. "A hall both vaster and deeper than these halls are. Since the world was, no light ever came there."

"That was not hid from you."

"Lord, I did not know it."

I answered thoughtlessly, "Glas Awyddn knew, before I knew myself. Truly, I remember little what I was until he came." I saw the hurt. "Until I saw you both," I said.

His stallion leapt forward.

The horses thundered along the worn stones of the causeway. The men rode four abreast, their long black lances outlined against the rock. But for all their number they might have been shadows. Though I knew it gave him no company, I urged my own mount again to his side. Without a word I reached across for his reins. He paid no heed to it. His eyes were empty. To the depth of his being there was loneliness. After a moment he turned to watch the old man leaning out of the tower. Something drew his eyes more fiercely to the ancient head.

"His mouth is cruel," Wyck said, "as cruel and sharp as an old cock salmon."

"Child, you have learned to look," I said gently. Before my own eyes the causeway was a blur of horses. I lifted my head. "That is more than can be said for these brave men. For they have never looked."

Free of the reins, the boy's hands trembled. He pressed them strengthlessly against the stallion's withers. If there were some warmth in that flesh, it passed to him. He said, "When I came to this place, I thought of nothing more than to ride with them, mounted on a horse such as I had never seen in dreams or racing the tide across the whole width of the bright sea floor, preparing for war."

"That war will come."

His head was lowered. "The Penandrun are very old," he said.

"I too am old."

For the first time he stared at me. "It is a child they look for."

"A boy," I said, "with the glamour of fire in him, fair

as good weather." I laughed. "Bright as the glow of gold."

Then sun, safe on its own high path, covered the lake with blazing light. On every side, as though the boundless sky were mirrored in the rock, the stones of the towers stretched away. In the brightness, in the heart of the burning, he saw, at the very last clearly, I was not there.

"Lord," he stammered, his voice so fragile I knew that it would break. "They will see . . ."

"Nothing," I answered him firmly, ". . . unless you mention it."

She reaches out to touch my arm and, not finding it, wakes instantly. The cool air of autumn drifts in through the window. A capricious breeze, but not unkind, it swirls over the risen flesh of her nipples. She has been dreaming and, turning her thin shoulders at the edge of sleep, has driven off the coverlet. For a moment she draws it back then sits up sharply. From that high place, through the oblong hole where the wind comes and goes as it pleases, immune to her governance, she can see the river licked up white under the stars. The room itself is dark. Even against her tongue I have had my will in that.

"Husband?" she says softly.

The chair by the doors is half in shadow, but now she sees no one is in it. Still, she is not frightened. Ever since our sons were nine-month born, came howling out of her like any other, with mannish hands and mannish feet, she seldom gives a thought to signs and portents. "This is a king's house," she is fond of saying. "A king's peace I shall have in it."

When I do not answer she climbs from the bed and irritably, without her covering, walks to the window. At first there is no sound, then quite close someone is talking. In the yard a guard is pacing. The breeze flutters past her, taking some of her resentment with it. She is nearly thirty-eight. The starlight silhouettes her figure. A bit of light slants across each breast as she turns back again. They are still full. In seventeen years she has not forgotten how to bargain with the dark.

"I have been dreaming," she says ruminatively.

"A stranger?" I ask from the chair, the face she cannot see mischievous.

"No stranger, husband," she answers. "It is your own sons I am thinking of." She heaves her thin shoulders, walking boldly toward where she has decided I must be.

"Woman, I warn you. I have lain with a hundred queens."

She laughs. "With their bones, to hear you talk of it."

I feel her breath. She is resolved, as much and as in many ways as her grand strapping father was, though through all the sorrowing days he marched with me across the cantreds, treading the muddy reaches of the Tywy and back to the valley's narrow end, he marshaled hosts. A girl, a woman now, as resolved and earnest as her father, neither discomfited nor shamed, she holds in front of me the breasts and belly that got our sons, as she has held them before the passing guard, though as yet, because I will not move, she does not know for certain I am here.

"Woman, I have dreamed myself."

Thinking surely now I must take hold of her, she does not reach out.

"Lord?"

"Before the sea was cold," I say, "before there was any land for it to roll against, across the stillness that was then, we faced each other, her face that was not a woman's yet—for there were no women until she decided she would be the first—that face intent and white on

mine, and mine that I myself had made so I could stare
at her, mine dark with shame, afraid now that I had
fashioned it that she would see its longing, our two
faces looked out and all we knew was fear."

Had she a gown to cover her, she would have had
some use for her small fingers, a seam to straighten,
some little fold to fasten back. Yet, knowing her worth,
she keeps them quiet on her thighs.

"Lord," she sighs, resentful and yet, perhaps, because she is used to this as well, amused. "Lord," in a
voice made almost tender, "what should you fear? Already I have made you sons."

The deeds of my youth are not now remembered. Nor
has any woman cared how once the darkness moved or
how I plucked the worlds from it. It is only because I
have not touched her, she reaches down.

"Not your sons," I whisper hoarsely. "It was myself I
meant to get reborn."

She does not listen. It is only because she has felt the
chair is empty that she screams.

The Penandrun were at work in their towers when
the sealmen came. The one who saw them did not think
to tell the rest. It was too great a labor to descend the
stairs, to cross the yards and mount again the endless
steps that circled up the inner walls. At the city's bright
enneadic heights there were too many cocklofts and
chambers. He did not move at all. Every now and then
his distant, little-seeing eyes would open. The sun
warmed his face. He felt only the creeping of his
ancient blood. Like all his brothers, he longed for the
days he had lost. The new thunder of horses on the
causeway brought nothing that had not already left him
discontented.

He knew exactly how the sealmen would look, their
lances discarded, locked away from them for the winter

while he taught them tales they saw no use to learn. He knew how they would whisper when he turned his back, how they would mutter when, in the midst of the song, his own deep boredom for that moment replaced with wonder, he saw the slopes and beaches swarm with men, saw the white bay filled with sails, the sealmen climbing naked from the sea.

Tywy, he thought.

But in this place the harbor was blue and tranquil, the only sound the commotion of horses. That was no more strange today than it had ever been nor any more worth his notice. He glanced down, the lines of his face unchanging. The same lances waved; the same green stallions trotted on the stones. Yet, just once, above the usual shouting a man called out to him.

"Grandfather!"

The old one cocked his head. He rubbed his eyes and cocked his head again.

The sealmen and their horses were gone, the causeway silent. He stared back at the room absently. Now, for some hours, the sun had left it. Without moving, he noticed his thin wrinkled fingers were white with frost, white as the morning, white, he recalled suddenly, as an eight-legged stallion. He raised his head. Though he had not moved for a very long time, he went to the stairs.

The tunnels were fair-sized but the sealmen were many. Yet as they rode, men turned aside, driving the horses under wide galleries of dark, polished stone, urging them to the left and right in the darkness under the walls. Wyck caught glimpses of their armor. He could not have found the way himself. On the plain the road had gone on before him, the mountain growing larger, drawing him onto it. Here there were too many passages, twisting, opening suddenly and blankly, and no ray of light marking one from the next. The men around him were nearly as indistinguishable. But he did not move his head. He was trying to remember the exact look on his face—the sun burning above him on the causeway—as it faded.

"There are deeper ways under this," Eachanhagen said. There were stairs and doorways now, below the arched ceiling, hollowed out in the deep mountain rock. He saw them dimly. A breath of chill air, escaping from the delvings, blew over his back. Eachanhagen's voice echoed. "The stells and the stables are below us," he said, "the grooms' halls and forges. There are others farther down."

Had he stopped to think, Wyck would have noticed that already they had descended well beneath the level of the lake. The passage plunged steeply. The cold air thickened and dripped. But he had felt no dread of the tunnels, had given no thought to them. Still, his hands trembled. He ran them cold on his forehead and into his hair.

"Someone must tell them," he said. His unhappy eyes found the unchanging eyes of the tall man beside him.

"Tell them what?"

"That their dreams are nothing."

Eachanhagen looked down at him. In his left hand, the sealman carried a high, smooth lance, its butt resting against the flank of his stallion. Its points were deadly. At a gallop he could drive them into a yard of wood. He was a fearsome man. And yet he had not forgotten the first morning he had ridden here, into a darkness unearthly and filled with the pounding of hooves. The boy was small. What chance has he, the man thought, against the things of his imagining?

The sealman smiled. "The tunnels open up to the

yards beyond," he said. "In a moment you will see the sun again."

But the ceilings lowered and the sealmen bent down, tipping their lances. The last gleamings faded. The horses tramped across darkness; the echoes fell farther back. The horsemen swept on and took no heed of them. Wyck heard their pace quickening. If the man heard him sobbing, he did not remark on it.

In time there was light again, a vague, dusty light softening the edges of the stone far ahead of them, then a slender crack that yawned, that grew wider until the advancing mouth of the tunnel filled with daylight. Then at last Wyck saw the hosts of men, the grooms and the scavengers, the fetchers and hardwaremen, streaming out of the holes and warrens, slamming the doors on their forges, shouting and pouring over the walls. A sealman raised his horn and blew. The sound rose above the thunder of feet on the gangways. Under the cavernous roof of tunnels the air rang with shouts. "Llugh!" the men yelled. They ran alongside the horses, their eyes darting from one man to the next.

The passage climbed swiftly. The first of the horsemen passed under the archway, into a yard opened up to the morning. The shouts of a greater host greeted them. The sound grew to a roaring. Another sound waited behind it, unused and impatient. Rank by rank the horsemen entered the yard, the sound growing restless, swelling when each new man came into the light, but lapsing back when the shadows had left him. Glas Awyddn passed beneath the stone's edge, Eachanhagen behind him. Just beyond the portal they halted. Above them, along the curving terraces carved into the rock, ten thousand figures stood, their shoulders rigid, their dark eyes flickering. Now, like the horseman, the host of men waited. Moved by the hush, a stallion whickered. A sealman patted his neck.

They saw the great horse as he broke from the portal. His white head was lifted, his head turning coldly. But the sound they had waited to make had died in their throats. It was so still they might have heard, even from far off, the flutter of the wind through the cloaks of the old ones looking down from their towers. The old ones themselves were silent: the horse was riderless.

Eachanhagen was the first to speak. No amazement rooted his tongue. He stood high in his stirrups. "He had come!" he shouted, shaking his fists at the ramparts and terraces. "The men with me rode with him. Here before you is the horse he rode. Have any seen the like of him?" He spat. "Who are you to question if in the tunnels he went his own way? Which of you would choose for him? Even now he speaks with the old ones."

Necks craned upward. And indeed in each tower the tall windows were empty, the old ones gone from them. The many faces of the hosts moved again, uneasily.

Eachanhagen put aside his lance. "Come then," he boomed. "Where are the grooms? Our horses have ridden long and are weary." He looked around him into the faces of the hosts. The silence made him shout again. But at last the captains called out. The stretch of waiting loosened. Once more a sealman lifted his horn. Before the high note ended a man leapt free of the walls. Another man followed. To the left a ramp of rough planking slid down into the yard. The grooms came running along it. "He is here," the grooms whispered. "These men have seen him. Soon enough, when he pleases, he will show himself." Discontented but knowing now what must surely come, the grooms went forth, spreading out among the horses, hailing the men they knew. All the way up to the high open windows, if there was not laughter, once again there was shouting.

The riders closest to Eachanhagen did not climb from their mounts. They looked up at the towers. But even to them the grooms came at last, albeit more slowly, for the great stallion, his head tossing, paced the ground in front of them. The sharp white sunlight danced on his back. The light dazzled the grooms.

But there was one who did not fear him. He came away from the wall, and the younger grooms made a path for him. Though one leg was lame, he walked quickly. He seemed nearer a hundred than fifty, but his brows were pointed and stiff and his beard was as red as a coal in a grate. He was groom master and dressed for his office, in a thick cloak of mixed wools, rachan-shaded and stained at the edge. A strange benevolence shone in his owlish round eyes as he came up to the stallion. Cooling, he reached for his muzzle.

The stallion drew back.

"Eachanhagen?" Glas Awyddn said.

"It is only fitting," the sealman answered. "Now he will be stabled apart, in a place that long has been kept for him."

The old man edged nearer. "May the god be my witness!" he cried. "In a hall to himself. And myself I will curry him. Alone I will do it. Though the old ones set me a hundred tasks, I will neglect them." His trembling fingers reached for the mane.

"It is your life if he is lamed," Glas Awyddn said.

"Truly," the old man said, "what is the life of a dead man?"

The boy came up, last, leading his stallion. Glas Awyddn saw he was watching.

"Go yourself," Glas Awyddn said to him. "See that all that is done is done with care." He had meant it as a gift. Yet, because he had dared not look at him further, he turned away. Only Eachanhagen watched after them, the old man and the boy, the great horse between

them, going back through the portal. The long face of
the sealman had hardened.

"The blame is not on us," he said, "but on yourself."

"There was always risk."

"Still, you tempt it."

The sun poured its fire on the center of the yard.
Directly overhead, it filled the cracks of the earth,
warming the cramped, exhausted sinews of the stallions. Under their mail the sealmen sweated. Only one
man felt the edge of the wind or remembered its
coldness. Glas Awyddn pulled his mantle over his neck.

"How will I keep the salmon from the falls?" he said.
"No more than that may I keep him, though once he
was dear to me."

Eachanhagen frowned. A groom was taking his stallion. "It was for Llugh to decide," he said.

Glas Awyddn sucked his breath through his teeth.

The great hall faced north and east. When he walked
into it Glas Awyddn saw the wide leaded windows
looking over the lake and, on the far side, under the
hills, the masts of the ships, like a forest of brown,
leafless trees sticking up in the harbor. The windows
went straight to the roofbeam, the ceiling arched and
tall, so that the ships themselves might have fitted
beneath it. The space between was swimming with
light.

He had come in at the front of the company,
Eachanhagen beside him. Despite the press of men,
Glas Awyddn stopped at the doors. His back straightened. Under the casements he saw a high platform,
carved from the rock. Broad stairs went up to it. On
either side of the steps were chairs, their arms studded
with bronze and inlaid with horn. He did not need to
count them. The nine were empty. But the floor was
crowded. At first, seeing so many, he did not under-

stand why there was quiet. The leather in his armor creaked. The hilt of his sword flashed gold in the sunlight.

A guard came forward. He was a big man. His seahair was russet; his eyes, in their anger, nearly as red. It was to Eachanhagen he spoke.

"I greet you," he said, "but it is a stranger's welcome you have from me. Well enough you know the law. Never before have you brought your weapons into the hall." He was not armed but, as though his size were all the shield and arms he needed, he stepped in front of them. The listeners leaned nearer.

"Why are you speaking law to me?" Eachanhagen said. "We learned war here. Now war has come to it." He smiled, a wolf's smile. Out of courtesy the guard smiled back. But the smile was thin, the smile of a man remembering pain. His voice sounded weary. He said, "Since I crossed the blood river, this law has stood."

"I do not fault it," Eachanhagen said. The sun on his armor brought out the scents of hair and sweat. The soldiers shifted. A heaviness clung to them. But then he laughed. "Truly," Eachanhagen said, "who would trust such men—crowded in one hall—with arms? Men without love, without mercy." He stared at them, looked hard into faces that neither looked away nor looked back.

The guard waited. He said, "Even as you said it, it was the law."

"It was made and now it is broken." Eachanhagen walked sharply past him. But before he beckoned his soldiers he turned. "This was their house and their law while they ruled it. We have no quarrel. Old men bring advice, sad tales, and laws." He had lifted his hand; they saw the length of the shining sword he had drawn with it. "The new king brings war."

The guard moved abruptly, but the tautness in his

face had changed to astonishment. "We are doing this," he said.

Eachanhagen's lips twisted back. "It is the tales."

"Sir?"

"They are happening."

Glas Awyddn shrugged. Without meaning, the words buzzed around him. He was staring across the guard's shoulder toward the gray windows, feeling how the brightness had gone from them. He was much too high, he decided, to hear voices. The wind whimpered on the ledges, scraping the stones. Only the thunder of wheels drifted up to him.

He made his way to the stairs and climbed the steep platform. The darkening clouds were piling up behind the hills. He looked down at the lake. Along the causeway he saw the line of wagons moving across from the harbor. With his good eye he tried to count the herds and flocks that were swept along with them, going in through the walls. He could not tally them. The seaglass was thick. Still his nostrils flared. Catching the bitter scent of sheep, he remembered that the dead were numberless. Seized with impatience, he turned his back.

Even unwatched, the flocks and the herdsmen came without pausing, swelling the city, filling the yards and stells with the damp, oily bodies of beasts and men. He could not deny their numbers, yet their coming had left him with a feeling of unbearable emptiness.

It was the waiting, he told himself. But he was thinking of the woman he had seen just once—now slid beyond recognition or imagining—coming out of the sea. It seemed a lifetime ago, yet she whose face he could not now remember remained with him. Neither young nor old, now without flesh, without even substance, she bound him. Without her, he realized, his

heart sinking, he was not, not himself surely but only
the Un-Man's shadow—Duinn, Lord of Tricks and Lies.

He ground his teeth. Even then, though he was lost
and nothing, he found a piece of a thing to chew on. He
held it in his jaws. Thin, it was like a thread of a
woman's hair.

The grooms were running about in confusion. The
tunnels were filled with wagons and sheep. On the
gangways the hostlers chattered like starlings. The gray
darkness, like a wind swollen and bristling with the
sounds of hooves and murmuring, rolled against him.
But when the light from the open yard had dimmed
and vanished, when the last thralls and housemen,
gone their own ways, had wormed again into the rock,
Wyck could still hear the stallion beside him. The
passage dipped lower. The floor was slippery and smelled.
Cobwebs tickled his face. Through the walls he could
hear the deep, muffled groaning of the lake. The stallion whickered, but now the sound comforted him,
easing his pain. The boy swallowed bravely.

He no longer tried to believe he would not ride him.
From the morning he had seen the great horse trotting
out from the old woman's wood he had known this. Yet
for the days and nights they had ridden through the
realm, through the strange quiet wood and out again
onto the plain, he had kept his heart closed to it. From
that morning, his hands—as though they knew him
better than his blood—had ached to touch him. His
eyes, by themselves, had slid across his coat, had
watched in sly wonder how at every stride each prodigious white hoof judged the ground. And yet all the
while he had dared not tell himself.

Unwanted now, the lord's ungentle face slipped into
his mind. He knew—had known before the boy, looking
elsewhere, had even attempted not to think. One shoul-

der shrugged. Glas Awyddn gave me leave, Wyck thought.
The floor was paved with harsh old stones. The boy was
almost running when the man, panting behind him,
caught his arm.

Beyond a black arch a faint light shone, a new light,
gentle as the light of dawn. The stallion walked into it.
Wyck would have followed, but the old man lunged
ahead. Boldly, though he was short of breath, he barred
the way.

"Hold, boy," he panted. "It is his hall. He must be
the first to enter it."

"I was told to go with you."

The old man grunted. He wheezed despairingly and
shook his head. "Your lord was no more pleased than I
to have you come."

The boy was silent. The hooves of the stallion did not
seem to clatter on the stones. They caught each other's
eyes just once, then Wyck edged by him.

It was as though a veil had parted, a veil he had
never known was there. He saw the shining walls,
rising clear and bright, but, though he ran his eyes over
them, he could find no breach or opening. His legs
shifted restlessly. There were no torches, and yet a light
that had no source was slowly filling the hall, flowing
steadily into it as though from emptiness. He did not
see the stallion.

The groom master moved behind him. "For a thousand years," he said, "this hall stood waiting. As patient
as I could be, though seldom in this place, I waited
with it."

Wyck turned. The man was bearing a bundle of loose
straw away from the wall.

"In all that time I have not learned myself," he said
glumly, not looking up, "what He will have need of. I
can only do what I have done and hope." He left the
straw drop to the floor and scattered it. Without

straightening, he mopped his forehead. His robe was open; Wyck saw the number of his arms. "Come," the man said, "if I must have you, I'll have as well your hand with this."

"You have hands enough."

"The work takes many."

The boy shrank back from him. "Lord," he said slowly, "twice already I have seen you, at the blood river and in the field, yet I do not know that work."

"How would a boy hear of it?" he said coldly. He lifted his head, plain as a farmer's and ruined with scars. "Yet it was no riddle. It is the first work that was ever done, though it is never finished. So I have kept at it." He reached again for the straw. A brightness filled the air in front of him. Wyck followed after.

"Still, I do not know it," he said.

"Dividing."

"What?"

"The wind in its quarters, the darkness from morning, a man—"

The boy was not listening. He was staring. Once more the eight white hooves of the stallion were trotting on the stones.

"He is here," the boy whispered, "but for a moment he was not." The man looked across at him, gauging the wonder in his bony face. Something changed in him.

"He rides with the sun," the old man said carefully. "So at least it is said." His lips parted, then closed again firmly as though he debated with himself. The straw was still in his hand. He straightened wearily. "Surely," he said, "he comes and goes as he pleases. And so he might. For he is free of everything except his will."

The boy cocked his head. "Yet if a man rode him," Wyck said softly, "could he be ridden there?"

"To what place?"

"Across the bright heavens—"

"He would have his death," the man said quickly. The cleft between the old red brows deepened. "And not the little death we know, but that beyond rebirth, which Duinn gives." Himself, he thought of the monstrous dark, the cold beyond bearing. For a moment, even in the light, he found he was shivering.

"But if there were a man—or even a boy—" Wyck went on eagerly, "who could not die?" He drew a swift, silent breath. His unlined, long face was beaming.

In the first hour of morning, when there was still darkness, the Penandrun sent a herald to Eachanhagen and to all of the chiefs of the sealmen in their scattered barracks under the walls. Eachanhagen was already wide awake. In truth he had been unable to sleep and had kept the watch himself, trying to wear out his impatience by pacing the stones. Toward morning he had gone out onto the dark platform overhanging the lake. Alone in the shadows he had waited, staring up at the towers. The chill water under him no longer seemed to knock at the walls. A less stubborn man might have noticed. He had been too filled with waiting to hear sounds that were not. But he saw the herald before the other man saw him.

"Has he been seen, man?" he yelled. "Has he called for us?"

"No," the herald answered him darkly. "It is the Penandrun who want you."

"Myself?"

The man's face hardened. "When have they ever wanted one of you?" he said. "Call your hosts and go to them."

Eachanhagen's lips were a savage line. "He has come," he said grimly and walked past him.

There were no lights in the yards, none in the

passages winding cold in the darkness, or in the deep stone cellars, none in the rooms without number that made up the holding. What light is there where no fires burn? There was only a sound, like the sea wind scraping the rock, only a whisper, like the seal's crying, filling the chambers where the lonely men slept. The heralds' eyes flickered. They banged open the doors.

"You brag a great deal about your skill in a battle you have never fought," the heralds called out loudly, making the sleeping men jump, their slack faces turn purple with rage. "To your feet, lads, and quickly," they shouted. "These old men do not lack wisdom. They will have you shame them when you come to land."

Nowhere is it different.

Cups and stools were thrown at the backs of the heralds, who, expecting little else, had, by a whisker, gotten themselves safely beyond the thick doors. The sealmen grumbled. But they reached for their boots. And in the end they went—for so the heralds had always summoned them—even eagerly, stretching their legs in the cold, striding off in the darkness. Over his shoulder a man with a piercing and lively eye grinned at his comrades. He had a sharp, ugly face but the harsh timbre of his voice had turned to wonder. "It is all right, then," he laughed. "We are not rousted for nothing."

Not that any, now within the walls, had seen him. But on the sea road they had passed him. The memory still haunted them. They stared at one another and in their death-filled faces each saw the same grave longing and delight. He was the Promised One.

In him the flame of life still burned, charmed and undiminished. Himself he knew no death, had never known it. His sea-black eyes, they had seen, had pride in them but no deeper shadow. Like no other king he had come to this place gladly, down to these brooding halls, unshaped as any child, without a wound.

He was a flame.

They looked at one another and in their eyes that neither fell nor grew strained they saw the chance the fire might catch with nearness. They were not men; they were eyes that tore holes in the darkness, waiting. So on the shrouded hill at Hwawl and Abereth the living men waited. Huddled near the piles of wood, no longer watching the great sparks fly against the winter's dark, they waited for dawn. On the beaches of Tywy, the cliffs behind them red with burning, the women looked at the sea.

The passage was narrow, the movement back and forth considerable. Glas Awyddn pressed himself along, then in through the doors. Many more were lumbering in in back of him. He allowed himself to be pushed onto one of the benches. He could hear the voice of Eachanhagen booming loudly out in the passage, reprimanding a groom. When he came in himself, climbing over the backs and shoulders of his men, a gust of laughter greeted him. Sullenly, awkward in front of their grinning, he ordered a man elsewhere and sat down at last, as inconspicuously as his size and his anger would let him, beside Glas Awyddn.

"You must hurry yourself hereafter," a man in front shouted back at him.

There was another gust of laughter.

Eachanhagen scowled but did not answer. His mouth tightened.

"It is ill done," he said to Glas Awyddn quietly. "He may have my share of this, if he wants it." His head bent forward. He sucked one of his blunt fingers.

"What is it?" Glas Awyddn asked.

"I do not know."

The wind brushed on the window glass. The sealmen waited. Gradually, as darkness was replaced with morning, they saw in disbelief it was snowing. They looked beyond the tall windows. Snow came swirling out of the sky like frosted breath. Deep as twilight it was filling the harbor. Against the storm the ships' naked rigging seemed draped with sails.

Glas Awyddn turned his back from the windows. He rubbed his cold arms.

"I have not seen Wyck," he said. He stopped abruptly. He felt a stiff wind moving over him.

As though on its own a wide panel swung out from the casement. But it was a man, without question, his shoulders bent beneath his cloak, who pushed it shut. He was old and hobbled. Wet flakes clung to his brows. He did not brush them out, did not notice them. He shook his damp cloak when he was only half out of it. When he had gotten himself free of it, he hung it from a carved peg on the wall.

"I had thought," he began. He paused, nodding to Eachanhagen and to one or two of the others formally, to Gwyn and to Annwn, who nodded back. "I had thought," he went on quietly, "you must have come."

Without his cloak his thinness showed painfully. He looked out sadly over the rows of men. His bloodless lips narrowed. "This year there are more of you," he said softly, in a voice that could scarcely be heard and yet needed to be no louder.

Because he had no hope of keeping silent, Eachanhagen turned his broad shoulders. "Old one," he murmured, "there were three that I found."

The sightless eyes did not appear to look.

In the hall there was a crowd of men and not one from whom the thing was hidden. But the men were quiet.

Eachanhagen frowned. His great voice, filling the

hall as the old one's had not, barely trembled. "He has come," he said.

The sealmen grinned. Already a few more standing.

"So they have always come," the old one whispered.

"No."

The old one turned to watch the snow make heavy curtains on the glass. His hand drifted upward, touching for a moment the lines of his mouth. "There is a boy," he said, "and in the deepest hall an eight-legged stallion." His face held a look of more than human weariness. "Even in the towers such things are heard." His deep old eyes looked back at Eachanhagen.

"I will tell you this," he said. "Before first light I went myself. Though in a thousand years I had not left these halls, I went out walking. In the darkness I stood on the quay." He stared, as though in wonder at himself. A strange, astonished anger moved his breath. "You have not been alone in waiting. Long we sought the river's mouth, the memory of the lost way back. Before the cold moon flew into the dark or the day star burned, we yearned to walk the stronger, clearer world again."

They saw the awful stillness in his face. He was looking past them as though their staring were as blank as all the years, as empty as the glass through which they saw the harbor fill with snow instead of light.

"Before there were dreams," he said, "or men to dream them, when there were yet no women growing pale with pain, no hot small arms reaching out in joy or grief for sons, alone, prowling the icy coast, we waited."

Eachanhagen faced him squarely. One of his hands was hidden in the thick of his mantle. His hot rage burned. "That waiting's done," he said.

"It is too soon."

"Lord, I rode with him."

The old one's breath hissed irritably between his

teeth. "In the spring," he said, "when the wind blows east across the waves." He stopped to moisten his lips. He paused as though, in thinking only, he could taste the foam, could feel at his back the east wind filling the sails. "Ships without number he will send against the land." He raised his head. "Bright ships, white as gulls, and many as the birds in April." He stared, his chilled voice lowering until it seemed no voice at all, only a sound the wind made. "I went to look myself," he said. "Those ships lay frozen in the ice."

Eachanhagen leaned forward. The years and the longing had not lessened his strength.

"Here in this hall!" Eachanhagen shouted.

"No. You have not listened." The old one stood quietly. "Once at Tywy," he said, "there was a man, gray-haired and grieving the death of a boy." His flesh was blistered and yellow. But though he saw poorly, he saw the huge man running, the bold legs leaping onto the dais. He was not surprised. With deep certainty, by heart, he knew the blade's sharpness.

When he had drawn it out, Eachanhagen lifted the stainless sword in the air in front of him. The taut muscles of his face broke into wonder. "I have done this," he whispered. "Once—"

"No," the old one said gently. "In the years that must come there is another—at Ormkill, before the king's chair. As well, it will be a boy they are fearing then." He smiled. "A boy on a stallion coming out of the sea."

In the hall there is silence. The old one does not falter. For a thousand years, alive in his memory, he has carried the wound.

He climbed into the tower alone. Through the little glassless windows he saw the roofs of the holding gleaming silver with starlight, saw the hushed yards standing dark and empty below him. The storm had blown off to the east. But the air was bitter. He drew the borrowed cloak about his thin shoulders.

"I cannot go," he had told them.

"Then whom shall we send?" they had asked helplessly. "Each of us has sworn already. Whole companies have trooped before them, swearing—all who saw him, on the sea road and the plain. Still they only whisper on about the spring."

The boy had straightened, his dark eyes distant as he met their own. "I would have sworn myself," he had told them softly. "With all I was, I would have sworn to him, not to some old men that I had seen him, that he was here with us, but to himself, to give my service." They had heard the stallion, disturbed by their pleading, moving in the hall beyond. They had wished themselves elsewhere. The boy's voice had caught. He had raised his prideful eyes to look at them. "Yet," he had said, "he would not have me."

They had sought him last, when there had been no man left who had not sworn, when all, though they had been grave and honest, had been met with mockery. They had not come gladly. They had no love for these deep halls. Better the upper yards and the winter winds that howled along the lake than the brooding depths, far under the walls, where the stallion laired, hidden in its gloom though himself he was a thing of light.

"Child," they had murmured, "there is no deceit in us. We have seen him though we are not believed."

"I know what you have seen," he had answered them. "It is well for you I will not go and swear to it."

But he had gone.

The worn steps climbed beyond his sight. On the stallion's back, he thought, already I would have sailed beyond the sea. He imagined the sprawling city growing small beneath. Like a fistful of crags, he thought, the harsh tides rushing over it until it seemed one speck lost in the waves, until even the earth itself seemed but one more darkness in between the stars.

He had begun to think.

He had not seen himself the sealmen climbing the tower to the old one's court. But he knew they went, knew they swore great oaths that they had seen him, though in the rooms and halls they searched he was not found. Word spread among the grooms, went as quickly as to any other to the groom master's ear. So Wyck had heard it though he had not left the stallion's hall. He sat and waited.

The old man dragged a score of fingers through his hair. "They had dreamed of the day that he would come," he said. "But in their dreams he led them from the hall."

The boy smiled grimly. "Then it was only dreams."

"No."

"And lies."

"No."

"But he is Duinn."

"He is a man—though he was the first who died, the first who ever found darkness. Though he opened the sea road that the dead might follow him—still he is a man."

The boy only half listened. Glas Awyddn's words came back to him. "Then we have all the more to fear," he said, repeating them, not yet guessing what they meant. He felt the breath of the stallion, felt the warmth of the muzzle searching his back. *Horse, Great Horse,* he thought, *I will come for you.*

He left the hall.

After a while it seemed the endless stairs might reach themselves to the winds above the sea. But there was a door at the end of them. Wyck reached out his hand for the latchring and pulled it back. A stench blew in his face.

He remembered the smell of the corpses. But there had been a fire in the old woman's hut, a flame that had flared in the darkness, a warmth that had held him. Here there was only cold. His nostrils wrinkled.

Night curled around him, night's blackness, windy and porous and filled with empty space. Beyond the doomed roof there was nothing but darkness. He pulled the cloak about his thin shoulders.

"You are the last," the voices out of the air said quietly. "Come then and swear."

Wyck craned his neck until he saw where the nine were sitting in the dark and silence, their faces motionless as faces stitched in tapestries. Each face was turned aside, showing a single edge, as though the mischance and confusion of all their years had been compressed and sharpened. Like figures in a tale, he thought, men of whom it was remembered only that they burned or drowned and nothing else. A smile he had never smiled came to his lips. "Come," they said again.

Wyck shook his head. "You have not believed them."

The nine looked across at him. They did not raise an eyelid.

"They are men," Wyck said, "who dwelt with you and listened, men who only gave back what you had promised them."

Nothing moved but his own quick breath. He felt their stillness and knew it gave him power over them. He grinned more broadly. Because there was strength in his neck, he lifted it.

"What do you want?" he said boldly.

"To hear you swear."

He drew another breath and loosed it. He watched

its warmth, white for a moment, turn into darkness. Yet he could breathe again.

"You would not believe," he said.

"Does that matter?"

That one he did not answer. The silence became deeper. The corpse smell ate at his thoughts, and yet he knew the darkness and emptiness were outside of him. Shut within his flesh, where they could not reach it, there was a warmth, a flame that spread and mingled with his blood, a flame that came of itself, with no accounting. He turned, his startled eyes seeking beyond them.

"You are here," he said.

His voice drifted, unanswered, into the night.

"May I see you?"

"No."

"Yet you are one of them."

Unmoved, I watched him.

"I was before they were," I said.

He looked away. "Lord, they are only shadows."

"Less perhaps. Yet why should you be surprised at that?"

"You let me think that they were real."

"You might have guessed. I barely gave them shapes or names, but set them in an outlandish court, beyond the world's edge, where the sea was dry."

I saw he wept.

"Child, it was never different. From the first the tale was mine. What voice had I to have them speak with but my own?"

He shook his head. Though he had no answer, I could feel the flames that licked at him.

"I would have sworn to you," he whispered.

"That was before you knew."

"Glas Awyddn swore."

"Child, I have many names. His was always one of

them. From the beginning we were bound. Once he had loved her. Once, when he had no thought of loving, had turned his heart from it, in the emptiness of the morning he looked out at the sea."

His fingers tightened on the edges of the cloak. So Yllvere had held the fabric of her gown, knotting it, when at Ormkill before the barons she had withheld my name. Even in the darkness the cloak was shining. He let it drop. "Lord," he said softly, "I would have loved."

I was silent. Though I had held the worlds between my jaws and crushed them, even from my mouth no words would come.

The black waves break on the headlands at Tywy. The cold rain blows in gusts through the hall; the standing walls echo. Across the backs of the corpses the nine have come walking, treading on what lies stiffening as men will cross a river on stones. They are weighed down with grief. The earth, for its thinness, will not hold them.

From my place in the rock I look down at them. There are no longer doors or a roof to keep them out.

"We bear our own witness," they murmur. "We are more than shadows."

"You are what you have always been," I say, "as I am."

They are not content. The wind wanders through them, lifting their hair.

"Brother," they whisper, "you might have welcomed him. Until you stiffened your neck, there never was a companion truer than Death, nor a lord more willing to take men to his service. Yet you met him with silence."

But my jaw is set. "How," I ask them, "through all the long years have you failed to know my heart?"

The rain shocks the earth, the icy rain filling up silence. The wind blows from sea, across from the island where over and over I have murdered and am slain. I climb down from the rock.

But when I have come at last to Ormkill, to the brow of the hill overlooking the river, the nine are ahead of me, waiting. Already in the darkness the women are burning the dead. So the nine must stand in the air, finding their shapes in the smoke and the cinders that leap from the fires. I hear them grumble.

"Lord," they say in one voice, "let us not go from one place to another, unknowing. Now, if it is your will, we will listen."

His own poor shadow, shaped by the starlight, fled ragged before him, ran down the worn steps, turning the circuits of the stairs just ahead of him, turning over and over until he knew—though his shame gave him strength—he would not overtake it. A sob rose from his throat. His swimming eyes blurred on the rock.

It had seemed so little.

Indeed it could not have been much, not to him to whom all must be given. Still the boy wept.

Caught by its brooch, the cloak flapped desperately over his shoulders. Though his flesh burned, he pulled the gilded cloth more securely about him. This only he gave me, he thought, gave me freely, with no other reason than the rain fell and I shivered. He remembered the rain splashing down on the deck of the ship. He remembered the shape of the man, gleaming and white, like a vast snow mountain set adrift in the sea. But the heart of the man, like the heart of a mountain, was silent. The boy turned his head.

When he made the last circuit, he came out into the yard opened up in the darkness. Men who had crowded onto platforms and walls moved their stiff faces. Their eyes were impatient with waiting. Their lips trembled.

Last they had sent him. Little he had seemed to them, not enough to do their bidding, a child while they were men. But they had sent him, despite their bafflement, though even as they had sworn the nine had mocked them. He was their one hope and their last.

But his eyes strained over their backs, looking past them to the post of a gate where the stairs sank away again under the walls. He lifted his neck. Despite the cold, his face was bathed with sweat.

Only Glas Awyddn moved. Meaning comfort, he put out his hand.

The boy shifted.

He had begun to think again and yet it was no different from the thought that had come to him over and over since the day he first walked from the old woman's hut and saw a stallion, without blemish, trotting out of the morning.

Horse, Great Horse, he thought.

He left them and went to the stairs.

The stallion was waiting.

Ahead of him the rock seemed to open. The harsh old walls parted. The brilliant hooves flew over them, spurning their hardness and bitterness, the cold beyond hope. Under his legs the great stallion climbed as the sun climbs, setting his hooves above the small, rotted towers. The dark rim of the sea was below him.

He was free. Yet he had found no comfort. He was free and therefore knew he was unwanted. Beyond the little darkened world, high over it where the darkness holds no human shape, in the silence that wears neither likeness nor majesty, the breath of flame filled him and he burned.

Thus ends the second book of the Finnbranch, which is called *Undersea*. The last is called *Winterking*.

Names

Like burrs old names get stuck to each other and to anyone who walks among them. I have not tried to change that. Nine tenths of the names I used I borrowed. But then, the old names never lived one life and died. Remembered and reborn, they have entered other tales. While it is impossible to explain quickly matters that were a thousand years in the telling, in each name some vital part has kept its life. Their strength is their own. But because some readers may have forgotten them and because now and then I have gone my own way, I have listed a few which may require identification.

Agravaine	an early name of Finn
Anu	the Great Mother, goddess of fertility and fire
Ar Elon	the last of the seal-lords, High King of the land between the seas
Badb	the crow of Anu who stole Finn's eye
Cerridwen	the hag of Tywy, mistress of the quern of time
Dagda	the High King of the gods

Duinn	Death's Lord, lord of the sea and the darkness
Eachanhagen	a captain of the sealmen
Finn	Ar Elon's heir, the son of Yllvere
Fir Dhearga	an early name of Mug Dafad
Géar	Finn's twin sister, daughter of Yllvere and Ar Elon, the mother of Llugh
Géar Finn	the two-horned mountain above Morrigan
Glas Awyddn	Lord of Tir na Trí Oileán, given armor by Géar
Grieve	Finn's youngest sister, the daughter of Yllvere and Urien
Gwen Gildrun	the god-tree, sometimes found in Anu's wood and sometimes not
Hren	the island where Finn murdered Ar Elon, the gateway to the Other World
Hwawl	a village along the river Undain
Kell	the race of witch women who once mated with the sealmen
Llugh	the Shining One, the son of Finn and Géar
Morrigan	the house where Finn grew to manhood
Mug Dafad	the "Servant of Sheep"
Mughain	title of the queen of Tywy
Njal	Finn's youngest son
Ormkill	the great hall that Ar Elon built on the hills above the river Undain
Penandrun	the nine lords of undersea
Redd Man	he is named elsewhere
Ryth	one of Finn's sisters, daughter of Yllvere and Urien

Sanngion	one of Finn's sisters, daughter of Yllvere and Urien
Tabak ap Ewyn	one of the many names of Ar Elon
Tech Duinn	the House of Duinn
Thigg	Ar Elon's steward who ruled in his place at Ormkill
Tir fo Thuinn	the "Land under the Waves"
Tywy	the women's holding on the coast across from Hren
Unn	Finn's queen
Urien	Yllvere's old husband, Finn's foster father
Vydd	Yllvere's older sister, Finn's aunt
Wyck	Glas Awyddn's dog boy
Yllvere	the mother of Finn

COMING IN NOVEMBER...
THE POWERFUL
CONCLUSION TO
THE FINNBRANCH
TRILOGY

WINTERKING
By Paul Hazel

A World Fantasy Award nominee. On sale in November wherever Bantam Spectra Books are sold.

SCIENCE FICTION FROM
HARRY HARRISON

BANTAM
SHOP-AT-HOME
C·A·T·A·L·O·G

Special Offer
Buy a Bantam Book
for only 50¢.

Now you can have Bantam's catalog filled with hundreds of titles plus take advantage of our unique and exciting bonus book offer. A special offer which gives you the opportunity to purchase a Bantam book for only 50¢. Here's how!

By ordering any five books at the regular price per order, you can also choose any other single book listed (up to a $4.95 value) for just 50¢. Some restrictions do apply, but for further details why not send for Bantam's catalog of titles today!

Just send us your name and address and we will send you a catalog!